ALSO BY EMILY ST. JOHN MANDEL

The Glass Hotel

Station Eleven

The Lola Quartet

The Singer's Gun

Last Night in Montreal

SEA *of* TRANQUILITY

Emily St. John Mandel was born in Canada and studied dance at The School of Toronto Dance Theatre. She is the author of *Last Night in Montreal*, *The Singer's Gun*, *The Lola Quartet*, *Station Eleven*, *The Glass Hotel* and *Sea of Tranquility*. She lives in New York City with her husband and daughter.

SEA

of

TRANQUILITY

Emily St. John Mandel

PICADOR

First published in the USA 2022 by Alfred A. Knopf,
a division of Penguin Random House LLC, New York

First published in the UK 2022 by Picador
an imprint of Pan Macmillan
The Smithson, 6 Briset Street, London EC1M 5NR
EU representative: Macmillan Publishers Ireland Ltd, 1st Floor,
The Liffey Trust Centre, 117–126 Sheriff Street Upper,
Dublin 1, D01 YC43
Associated companies throughout the world
www.panmacmillan.com

ISBN 978-1-5290-8350-7

3 5 7 9 8 6 4 2

A CIP catalogue record for this book is available from the British Library.

Printed and bound by CPI Group (UK) Ltd, Croydon, CR0 4YY

Visit **www.picador.com** to read more about all our books
and to buy them. You will also find features, author interviews and
news of any author events, and you can sign up for e-newsletters
so that you're always first to hear about our new releases.

For Cassia and Kevin

Contents

Remittance /

1912

1

Edwin St. John St. Andrew, eighteen years old, hauling the weight of his double-sainted name across the Atlantic by steamship, eyes narrowed against the wind on the upper deck: he holds the railing with gloved hands, impatient for a glimpse of the unknown, trying to discern something—anything!—beyond sea and sky, but all he sees are shades of endless grey. He's on his way to a different world. He's more or less at the halfway point between England and Canada. *I have been sent into exile,* he tells himself, and he knows he's being melodramatic, but nonetheless there's a ring of truth to it.

Edwin's ancestors include William the Conqueror. When Edwin's grandfather dies, his father will become an earl, and Edwin went to two of the best schools in the country. But there was never much of a future for him back in England. There are very few professions that a gentleman can take up, and none of them are of interest to Edwin. The family estate is destined to go to his oldest brother, Gilbert, so he stands to inherit nothing. (The middle brother, Niall, is in Australia already.) Edwin might have clung to England a little longer, but he holds secretly radical views which emerged unexpectedly at a dinner party, thus speeding up his fate.

In a flash of wild optimism, Edwin has his occupation recorded as "farmer" on the ship's manifest. It occurs to him later, in a contemplative moment out on deck, that he's never so much as touched a spade.

2

In Halifax he finds lodging by the port, a boardinghouse where he's able to secure a corner room on the second floor, overlooking the harbour. He wakes that first morning to a wonderfully lively scene outside his window. A large merchant ship has arrived, and he's close enough to hear the jovial curses of the men unloading barrels and sacks and crates. He spends much of that first day gazing out the window, like a cat. He planned to go west immediately, but it's so easy to linger in Halifax, where he falls prey to a personal weakness he's been aware of all his life: Edwin is capable of action but prone to inertia. He likes sitting by his window. There's a constant movement of people and ships. He doesn't want to leave, so he stays.

"Oh, just trying to puzzle out my next move, I suppose," he says to the proprietor, when she makes gentle inquiries. Her name is Mrs. Donnelly. She's from Newfoundland. Her accent confounds him. She sounds like she's from Bristol and also from Ireland, simultaneously, but then sometimes he hears Scotland. The rooms are clean and she's an excellent cook.

Sailors pass by his window in jostling waves. They rarely look up. He enjoys watching them but dares not make any movement toward them. Besides, they have each other. When drunk they put their arms around one another's shoulders and he feels a piercing envy.

(Could he go to sea? Of course not. He discards the idea as soon as it arises. He once heard of a remittance man who reinvented himself as a sailor, but Edwin's a man of leisure through and through.)

He loves watching the boats come in, steamships pulling into the harbour with an aura of Europe still clinging to their decks.

He takes walks in the mornings and again in the afternoons. Down to the harbour, out to quiet residential areas, in and out of little shops under the striped awnings on Barrington Street. He likes to ride the electric streetcar to the end of the line, and then come back, watching the shift from small houses to larger houses to the commercial buildings downtown. He likes buying things that he doesn't especially need: a loaf of bread, a postcard or two, a bouquet of flowers. This could be a life, he finds himself thinking. It could be as simple as this. No family, no job, just a few simple pleasures and clean sheets to fall into at the end of the day, a regular allowance from home. A life of solitude could be a very pleasant thing.

He begins buying flowers every few days, which he places on his dresser in a cheap vase. He spends a long time gazing at them. He wishes he were an artist, to draw them and in so doing to see them more clearly.

Could he learn to draw? He has time and money. It's as good an idea as any. He makes inquiries with Mrs. Donnelly, who makes inquiries with a friend, and a short time later Edwin is in the parlour of a woman who trained as a painter. He spends quiet hours sketching flowers and vases, learning the fundamentals of shading and proportion. The woman's name is Laetitia Russell. She wears a wedding ring, but the location of her husband is unclear. She lives in a tidy wooden house with three children and a widowed sister, an unobtrusive chaperone who knits endless scarves in a corner of the room, so that for the rest of his life Edwin associates drawing with the clicking of knitting needles.

He's been living at the boardinghouse for six months when Reginald arrives. Reginald, he can tell at once, is not prone to inertia. Reginald has immediate plans to go west. He's two years older than Edwin, a fellow old Etonian, third son of a viscount, and his eyes are beautiful, a deep greyish blue. Like Edwin, his plans involve establishing himself as a gentleman farmer, but unlike Edwin, he's actually taken steps to achieve this and has been corresponding with a man who wishes to sell a farm in Saskatchewan.

"Six months," Reginald repeats at breakfast, not quite believing it. He stops spreading jam on his toast for a moment, seemingly unsure if he heard correctly. "Six *months*? Six months *here*."

"Yes," Edwin says lightly. "Six very agreeable months, I might add." He tries to catch Mrs. Donnelly's eye, but she's focusing intently on pouring tea. She thinks he's a little touched, he can tell.

"Interesting." Reginald spreads jam on his toast. "I don't suppose we're hoping to be called home, are we? Clinging to the edge of the Atlantic, staying as close as we can to king and country?"

This stings a little, so when Reginald lights out for the west the following week, Edwin accepts an invitation to join him. There's pleasure in action, he decides, as the train leaves the city. They've booked first-class passage on a delightful train that features an onboard post office and barbershop, where Edwin writes a postcard to Gilbert and enjoys a hot shave and a haircut while watching the forests and lakes and small towns slip past the windows. When the train stops at Ottawa he doesn't disembark, just stays on board, sketching the lines of the station.

The forests and lakes and small towns subside into plains. The prairies are initially interesting, then tedious, then unsettling.

There's too much of them, that's the problem. The scale is wrong. The train crawls like a millipede through endless grass. He can see from horizon to horizon. He feels terribly overexposed.

"This is the life," Reginald says, when at last they arrive, standing in the doorway of his new farmhouse. The farm is a few miles outside Prince Albert. It is a sea of mud. Reginald purchased it, sight unseen, from a disconsolate Englishman in his late twenties—another remittance man, Edwin can't help but suspect—who's thoroughly failed to make a go of it here and is headed back east to take a desk job in Ottawa. Reginald is very carefully not thinking about this man, Edwin can see that.

Can a house be haunted by failure? When Edwin steps through the door of the farmhouse, he feels immediately ill at ease, so he lingers out on the front porch. It's a well-built house—the previous owner was well-funded once—but the place is unhappy in a way that Edwin can't entirely explain.

"There's . . . a lot of sky here, isn't there?" Edwin ventures. And a lot of mud. Really an astonishing amount of mud. It glitters under the sun as far as he can see.

"Just wide-open spaces and fresh air," Reginald says, gazing out at the horrifically featureless horizon. Edwin can see another farmhouse, far away, hazy with distance. The sky is aggressively blue. That night they dine on buttered eggs—the only thing

Reginald knows how to cook—and salt pork. Reginald seems subdued.

"I suppose it's quite hard work, farming?" he says, after a while. "Physically taxing."

"I suppose so." When Edwin imagined himself in the new world, he always saw himself in his own farm—a verdant landscape of, well, of some unspecified crop, tidy but also vast—but in truth he never thought much about what the work of farming might actually entail. Taking care of horses, he supposes. Doing a bit of gardening. Digging up fields. But then what? What do you actually do with the fields, once you've dug them up? What are you digging for?

He feels himself teetering on the edge of an abyss. "Reginald, my old friend," he says, "what does a fellow have to do to get a drink around here?"

"You *reap*," Edwin says to himself, on his third glass. "That's the word for it. You dig up the fields, you sow things in the fields, then you reap." He sips his drink.

"You reap what?" Reginald has a pleasant way about him when he's drunk, as if nothing could possibly offend him. He's been leaning back in his chair, smiling into the empty air.

"Well, that's just it, isn't it," Edwin says, and pours himself another glass.

3

After a month of drinking, Edwin leaves Reginald on his new farm and continues west to meet up with his brother Niall's school friend Thomas, who entered the continent via New York City and sped west immediately. The train through the Rocky Mountains takes Edwin's breath away. He presses his forehead to the window, like a child, and openly gapes. The beauty is overwhelming. He maybe took the drinking a little far, back in Saskatchewan. He'll be a better man in British Columbia, he decides. The sunlight hurts his eyes.

After all that wild splendour, it's an odd jolt to find himself in Victoria, in those tamed and pretty streets. There are Englishmen everywhere; he steps out of the train and the accents of his homeland surround him. He could stay here for a while, he thinks.

. . .

Edwin finds Thomas in a tidy little hotel in the city centre, where Thomas has taken the best room, and they order tea with scones in the restaurant downstairs. They haven't seen one another in three or four years, but Thomas has changed very little. He has the same reddish complexion he's had since childhood, that perpetual impression of just having stepped in off the rugby pitch. He's trying to become a member of the Victoria business community, but he's vague on what kind of business he wants to be in.

"And how's your brother?" Thomas asks, changing the subject. He means Niall.

"Making a go of it in Australia," Edwin says. "He seems happy enough, judging by his letters."

"Well, that's more than most of us can say," Thomas says. "No small thing, happiness. What's he doing down there?"

"Drinking away his remittance money, I'd imagine," Edwin says, which is ungentlemanly but also the probable truth. They have a table by the window, and his gaze keeps drifting to the street, the shop fronts, and—visible in the distance—the unfathomable wilderness, dark towering trees crowding in around the periphery. There's something ludicrous about the idea that the wilderness belongs to Britain, but he quickly suppresses this thought, because it reminds him of his last dinner party in England.

4

The last dinner party began smoothly enough, but trouble started when the conversation turned, as ever and always, to the unimaginable splendour of the Raj. Edwin's parents were born in India, Raj babies, English children raised by Indian nannies—"If I hear one more word about her goddamned ayah," Edwin's brother Gilbert muttered once, never finishing the thought—and raised on tales of an unseen Britain that, Edwin couldn't help but suspect, had been slightly disappointing when they first laid eyes on it in their early twenties. ("More rain than I'd expected," was all Edwin's father would say on the matter.)

There was another family at that last dinner party, the Barretts, of similar profile: John Barrett had been a commander in the Royal Navy, and Clara, his wife, had also spent her first few years in India. Their eldest son, Andrew, was with them. The

Barretts knew that British India was an inevitable detour in any evening spent with Edwin's mother, and as old friends, they understood that once Abigail got the Raj out of her system, conversation could move on.

"You know, I so often find myself thinking of the beauty of British India," his mother said. "The colours were remarkable."

"The heat *was* rather oppressive, though," Edwin's father said. "That's one thing I didn't miss, once we came here."

"Oh, I never found it *terribly* oppressive." Edwin's mother had a far-off look that Edwin and his brothers called her British India expression. There was a haziness about her that meant she was no longer with them; she was riding an elephant or strolling through a garden of verdant tropical flowers or being served cucumber sandwiches by her goddamned ayah or something, who knows.

"Nor did the natives," Gilbert said mildly, "but I suppose that climate's not for everyone."

What inspired Edwin to speak just then? He found himself dwelling on the matter years later, at war, in the terminal horror and boredom of the trenches. Sometimes you don't know you're going to throw a grenade until you've already pulled the pin.

"Evidence suggests they feel rather more oppressed by the British than by the heat," Edwin said. He glanced at his father, but his father seemed to have frozen, his glass halfway between the table and his lips.

"Darling," said his mother, "whatever can you mean?"

"They don't want us there," Edwin said. He glanced around

the table, at all the silent staring faces. "Not a great deal of ambiguity on that point, I'm afraid." He listened to his own voice as
if from some distance away, with wonderment. Gilbert's mouth
had fallen open.

"Young man," his father said, "we have brought nothing but
civilization to these people—"

"And yet one can't help but notice," Edwin said, "that on bal-
ance, they rather seem to prefer their own. Their own civilization, that is. They managed quite well without us for some time,
didn't they? Several thousand years, wasn't it?" It was like being
strapped to the roof of a runaway train! He actually knew very
little about India, but he remembered having been shocked as a
boy by accounts of the 1857 rebellion. "Does anyone want us
anywhere?" he heard himself ask. "Why do we assume these far-
flung places are ours?"

"Because we *won* them, Eddie," Gilbert said, after a brief
silence. "One assumes that the natives of England were perhaps
not unanimously delighted by the arrival of our twenty-second
great-grandfather, but, well, history belongs to the victors."

"William the Conqueror was a thousand years ago, Bert.
Surely we might strive to be somewhat more civilized than the
maniacal grandson of a Viking raider."

Edwin stopped talking then. Everyone at the table was staring
at him.

"'The maniacal grandson of a Viking raider,'" Gilbert repeated softly.

"Although one should be grateful, I suppose, that we're a

Christian nation," Edwin said. "*Imagine* what a bloodbath the colonies would be if we weren't."

"Are you an atheist, Edwin?" Andrew Barrett inquired, with genuine interest.

"I don't quite know what I am," Edwin said.

The silence that followed was possibly the most excruciating of Edwin's life, but then his father began speaking, very quietly. When Edwin's father was furious, he had a trick of beginning speeches with a half-sentence, to catch everyone's attention. "Every advantage you've ever had in this life," his father said. Everyone looked at him. He began again, in trademark fashion, only slightly louder, and with deadly calm: "Every advantage you've ever had in this life, Edwin, has derived in some manner or another from the fact of your being descended from, as you so eloquently put it, the *maniacal grandson of a Viking raider.*"

"Of course," Edwin said. "It could be so much worse." He raised his glass. "To William the Bastard."

Gilbert laughed, in a nervous way. No one else made a sound.

"I do beg your pardon," Edwin's father said to their guests. "One might reasonably mistake my youngest son for a grown man, but it seems he's still a child. To your room, Edwin. We've heard quite enough for one evening."

Edwin rose from the table with great formality, said, "Good night, everyone," went to the kitchen to request that a sandwich be delivered to his room—the main course hadn't yet been served—and then retired to await his sentence. It came before midnight, with a knock on the door.

"Come in," he said. He'd been standing by the window, staring fretfully out at the movements of a tree in the wind.

Gilbert came in, closed the door behind him, and sprawled into the ancient stained armchair that was among Edwin's most treasured possessions.

"Quite the performance, Eddie."

"I don't know what I was thinking," said Edwin. "Actually, no, that's not true. I do know. I am absolutely certain there was not a single thought in my head. It was like a kind of void."

"Are you unwell?"

"Not at all. Never better."

"It must have been rather thrilling," Gilbert said.

"It was, actually. I won't say I regret it."

Gilbert smiled. "You're to go to Canada," he said gently. "Father's making arrangements."

"I was always going to go to Canada," Edwin said. "It's planned for next year."

"Now you're to go a little sooner."

"How much sooner, Bert?"

"Next week."

Edwin nodded. He felt a touch of vertigo. There had been a subtle shift in the room's atmosphere. He was going to go forth into an incomprehensible world and the room was already receding into the past. "Well," Edwin said, after a moment, "at least I'll still be on a different continent to Niall."

"You're at it again," Gilbert said. "Do you just say whatever comes into your head now?"

"I recommend it."

"We can't all be so careless, you know. Some of us have responsibilities."

"By which you mean a title and an estate to inherit," Edwin said. "What a terrible fate. I'll weep for you later. Will I receive the same remittance as Niall?"

"A little more. Niall's is just meant to support him. Yours comes with conditions."

"Tell me."

"You're not to come back to England for a while," Gilbert said.

"Exile," Edwin said.

"Oh, don't be melodramatic. You were always going to go off to Canada, as you said."

"But how long's a while?" Edwin turned away from the window to stare at his brother. "I'd thought I could go to Canada for a time, establish myself somehow, and then come home at regular intervals for visits. What did Father say, exactly?"

"I'm afraid the phrase that sticks in memory is 'tell him he's to stay the hell out of England.'"

"Well, that's rather . . . unambiguous."

"You know how Father is. And of course Mother is going along with it." Gilbert stood, and paused for a moment by the door. "Just give them time, Eddie. I'd be astonished if your exile were permanent. I'll work on them."

5

The trouble with Victoria, in Edwin's eyes, is that it's too much like England without actually being England. It's a far-distant simulation of England, a watercolour superimposed unconvincingly on the landscape. On Edwin's second night in the city, Thomas takes him to the Union Club. It's enjoyable at first, a shot of home, pleasant hours slipping past in the company of a few other old boys from the homeland and some truly exceptional single-malt scotch. Some of the older men have been in Victoria for decades, and Thomas seeks out their company. He stays close, asks their opinions, listens seriously to them, flatters them. It's embarrassing to watch. Thomas is clearly hoping to establish himself as a steady kind of man with whom one might wish to go into business, but it's obvious to Edwin that the older men are only being polite. They're not interested in outsiders, even outsiders from the correct country, with the correct ancestors and the correct accent, who've gone to the correct school. It's a closed society that admits Thomas only on the periphery. How long will Thomas have to stay here, circling around inside this clubhouse, before they'll accept him? Five years? Ten? A millennium?

Edwin turns his back on Thomas and goes to the window. They're on the third floor, with a view of the harbour, and the last light is fading from the sky. He feels restless and ill at ease. Behind him, men are relating tales of sporting triumphs and uneventful voyages by steamship to Quebec City, Halifax, and New York. "Would you believe," an arrival at the latter port is saying, somewhere behind him, "my poor mother was under the impression that New York was still part of the Commonwealth?"

Time passes; night falls over the harbour; Edwin rejoins the other men.

"But the unfortunate truth of the matter," one says, in the depths of a conversation about the importance of being an adventuring sort, "is we've no real future back in England, have we?"

A pensive silence falls over the group. These men are second sons, one and all. They are ill-prepared for a working life and will inherit nothing. To his own great surprise, Edwin raises a glass.

"To exile," he says, and drinks. There are disapproving murmurs: "I would hardly call this *exile*," someone says.

"To building a new future, gentlemen, in a new and far-distant land," says Thomas, ever the diplomat.

. . .

Later, Thomas finds him standing by the window.

"You know," he says, "I may have heard something or other in passing about a dinner party, but I'm not sure I quite believed it till now."

"I'm afraid the Barretts are incorrigible gossips."

"I think I've had about enough of this place," Thomas says. "I thought I could make a go of it here, but if you're going to leave England, surely there's something to be said for actually leaving England." He turns to face Edwin. "I've been thinking about going north."

"How far north?" Edwin is beset by a worrisome vision of igloos on the frozen tundra.

"Not very far. Just up Vancouver Island a little."

"You have prospects there?"

"Specifically, my friend's uncle's timber company," Thomas says. "But in the abstract, wilderness. Isn't that why we're here? To leave a mark on wilderness?"

What if one wanted to disappear into wilderness instead? A strange thought on a northbound boat a week later, steaming up the broken coast of the west side of Vancouver Island. A landscape of sharp beaches and forest, mountains rising up behind. Then all at once the broken rocks subside into a white-sand beach, the longest Edwin has ever seen. He sees villages on the shore, smoke rising, those wooden columns with wings and painted faces—totem poles, he remembers now—erected here and there. He doesn't understand them and therefore finds them menacing. After a long time the white sand subsides into rocky crags and narrow inlets again. Every so often he sees a canoe in the distance. What if one were to dissolve into the wilderness like salt into water. He wants to go home. For the first time, Edwin begins to worry about his sanity.

The passengers on the boat: three Chinese men going to work in the cannery, a very tense young woman of Norwegian origin travelling to join her husband, Thomas and Edwin, the captain and two Canadian crewmen, all in the company of barrels and sacks of supplies. The Chinese men talk and laugh in their own language. The Norwegian woman stays in her cabin except for meals, and never smiles. The captain and crew are cordial but uninterested in talking to Thomas and Edwin, so Thomas and Edwin spend most of their time together up on deck.

"What those utterly inert fellows in Victoria don't quite understand," Thomas says, "is that the entirety of this land is here for the taking." Edwin glances at him, and sees into the future: since Thomas was rejected by the Victoria business community, he'll spend the rest of his life railing against them. "They're ensconced in their very English city, and, look, I do understand the appeal, but we have an opportunity here. We can create our own world in this place." He drones on about empire and opportunity while Edwin gazes out over the water. The inlets and coves and little islands are on their starboard side, and just beyond them rises the immensity of Vancouver Island, its forests ascending into mountains whose summits are lost in low cloud. On the port side, where they're standing, the ocean extends uninterrupted until, as far as Edwin can figure it, the coast of Japan. He has the same queasy sense of overexposure that he felt on the prairies. It's a relief when the boat finally makes a slow right turn and begins travelling up an inlet.

They reach the settlement of Caiette in the early evening. There isn't much to it: a pier, a small white church, seven or eight houses, a rudimentary road that leads up to the cannery and the logging camp. Edwin stands by the pier with his steamer trunk beside him, at a loss. This place is precarious, that's the only word for it. It's the lightest sketch of civilizations, caught between the forest and the sea. He doesn't belong here.

"That bigger building up there's a boardinghouse," the captain says kindly to Edwin, "if you wanted to stay here for a spell, get your bearings."

It's troubling to realize he's so obviously lost. Thomas and Edwin walk up the hill together to the boardinghouse and secure rooms on the upper floor. In the morning Thomas departs for the logging camp, while Edwin slips immediately into the same stasis that overcame him in Halifax. It isn't quite listlessness. He makes a careful inventory of his thoughts and decides that he isn't unhappy. He just desires no further movement, for the time being. If there's pleasure in action, there's peace in stillness. He spends his days walking on the beach, sketching, contemplating the sea from the porch, reading, playing chess with other boarders. After a week or two, Thomas gives up trying to persuade him to come to the logging camp.

Edwin is astonished by the beauty of this place. He likes to sit on the beach, and just gaze out at the islands, little tufts of trees rising out of the water. Canoes pass by sometimes, on unknowable errands, and the men and women in the boats sometimes ignore him and sometimes stare. Larger boats come in at regular intervals, bringing men and supplies for the cannery and the camp. Some of them know how to play chess, which is one of Edwin's great pleasures. He's never been very good at chess, but he enjoys the sense of order in the game.

"What are you doing here?" they sometimes ask.

"Oh, just contemplating my next move, I suppose," he always replies, or words to that effect. He has a sense of waiting for something. But what?

6

On a sunny morning in September, he's out for a walk when he comes upon two Indigenous women laughing on the beach. Sisters? Good friends? They speak in a rapid language unlike anything he's ever heard, a language punctuated by sounds he can't imagine being able to replicate, let alone render in the Roman alphabet. Their hair is long and dark, and when one of them turns her head, light glances off a pair of enormous shell earrings. The women are wrapped in blankets against a cold wind.

They fall silent and watch him as he approaches.

"Good morning," he says, and touches the brim of his hat.

"Good morning," one replies. Her accent has a beautiful lilt. Her earrings hold all the colours of the dawn sky. Her companion, whose face bears a scattering of smallpox scars, just looks at him and says nothing. This isn't out of keeping with Edwin's experience of Canada—if anything, he reflects, it would come as the shock of his life if after half a year in the New World he were to find himself suddenly able to charm the locals—but the flat uninterest of the women's gaze is unnerving. This is a moment, he realizes, when he could express his views on colonization to people on the other side of the equation, so to speak, but he can't think of anything to say that doesn't sound absurd under the circumstances—if he tells them he believes colonization to be abhorrent, surely the logical next question will be *Then what are you doing here?*—so he says nothing further, and then they're behind him and the moment has passed.

He keeps walking, and then at some distance, still feeling their eyes on his back and wishing to convey an impression of having some sort of important errand to attend to, he turns toward the wall of trees. He never goes into the forest, because he's afraid of bears and cougars, but now it holds a strange appeal. He'll step in a hundred paces, he decides, no more. Counting off a hundred paces might calm him—counting has always calmed him—and if he walks straight for the full hundred then surely he can't get lost. Getting lost is death, he can see that. No, this whole place is death. No, that's unfair—this place isn't death, this place is indifference. This place is utterly neutral on the question of whether he lives or dies; it doesn't care about his last name or where he went to school; it hasn't even noticed him. He feels somewhat deranged.

7

The gates of the forest. The phrase comes immediately to mind, but Edwin's not sure where he picked it up. It sounds like something from a book he might have read as a boy. The trees here are old, and enormous. It's like stepping into a cathedral, except the underbrush is so thick that he has to fight his way through. He stops a few paces in. He sees a maple tree just ahead, large enough that it's created its own clearing, and that seems like a pleasant destination—he'll walk to the maple tree, he decides, he'll step out of the underbrush and linger a moment, then he'll go back to the beach immediately and never enter the forest again. This is an adventure, he tells himself, but it doesn't feel like an adventure. Mostly it feels like being slapped in the face with salal branches.

He fights his way through to the maple. It's quiet here, and he has a sudden certainty that he's being watched. He turns, and there—as incongruous as an apparition—is a priest, standing no more than a dozen yards away. He's older than Edwin, perhaps in his early thirties, and has very short black hair.

"Good morning," Edwin says.

"Good morning," the priest says, "and forgive me, I didn't mean to startle you. I like to walk here on occasion." There's something about his accent that eludes Edwin—it's not quite British, but not quite anything else. He wonders if the man's from Newfoundland, like his landlady back in Halifax.

"It does seem a peaceful destination," Edwin says.

"Quite so. I won't intrude on your contemplation, I was just on my way back to the church. Perhaps you'll stop in later."

"The church at Caiette? But you're not the usual priest," Edwin says.

"I'm Roberts. Filling in for Father Pike."

"Edwin St. Andrew. Pleased to meet you."

"Likewise. Good day."

The priest seems no more practised at walking through under-brush than Edwin. He crashes away between the trees, and within minutes Edwin is alone again, gazing up at the branches. He steps forward—

8

—into a flash of darkness, like sudden blindness or an eclipse. He has an impression of being in some vast interior, something like a train station or a cathedral, and there are notes of violin music, there are other people around him, and then an incomprehensible sound—

9

When he returns to his senses he's on the beach, kneeling on hard stones, vomiting. He has a vague memory of having fought his way out of the forest in a blind panic, a nightmare of shadow and blurred green, branches lashing his face. He rises shakily, and walks to the water's edge. He wades in up to his knees—the shock of cold is wonderful, it's the thing that will restore his sanity—and kneels to wash vomit from his face and shirt, then a wave knocks him over, so that by the time he stands he's choking on seawater and soaked through and through.

He's alone on the beach now, but he sees movement among the buildings of Caiette, in the middle distance. The priest disappearing into the white church on the hill.

10

When Edwin reaches the church, the door is ajar, and the room is empty. The door behind the altar is open too, and through it he sees a few gravestones in the green quiet of the tiny cemetery. He slips into the last row of pews, closes his eyes, and rests his head in his hands. The building is so new that the church still holds the fragrance of freshly cut wood.

"Did you fall in the ocean?"

The voice is gentle, the accent still indecipherable. The new priest—Roberts, he remembers—stands at the end of his pew.

"I knelt in the water. To wash vomit from my face."

"Are you unwell?"

"No. I . . ." It seems silly now, and a little unreal. "I thought I saw something in the forest. After I saw you. I heard something. I don't know. It seemed . . . supernatural." The details are already slipping away from him. He walked into the forest, and then what? He remembers darkness; notes of music; a sound he couldn't identify; all of it over in a heartbeat. Did it really happen?

"May I sit with you?"

"Of course."

The priest sits beside him. "Would it help to unburden yourself?"

"I'm not Catholic."

"I'm here to serve everyone who walks through those doors."

But the details are already fading. In the moment, the strangeness Edwin encountered in the forest was utterly destabilizing, but now he finds himself thinking of a particularly bad morning at school. He was nine, maybe ten, and he realized that he couldn't read the words in front of him, because the letters were wriggling into incoherence and there were spots swimming in his vision. He stood from his desk to ask to go see the matron, and he fainted. Fainting was darkness, but also sound: a murmuring and chirping like a chorus of birds, a blank void followed rapidly by an impression of being comfortably at home in bed—wishful thinking on the part of his subconscious, presumably—and then he woke into utter silence. Sound returned gradually, like someone turning a dial, silence fading into clamour and racket, the exclamations of other boys and the rapid steps of the approaching teacher—"Stand up, St. Andrew, no more malingering"—and was the moment just now in the forest really so different?

There were sounds, he reasons, and darkness, just like in that first instance. Perhaps he just fainted.

"I thought I saw something," Edwin says slowly, "but as I say it, I realize that perhaps I didn't."

"If you did," Roberts says gently, "you wouldn't be the first."

"What do you mean?"

"It's just, I've heard stories," the priest says. "That is, one hears stories."

This clumsy amendment strikes Edwin as a kind of camouflage, Roberts changing his patterns of speech to sound more English. More like Edwin. There's a wrongness about the man that Edwin can't entirely pinpoint.

"If I may ask, Father, where are you from?"

"Far away," the priest says. "Very far away."

"Well, that's all of us, isn't it," Edwin says, a little irritably. "Excepting the natives, of course. When we met in the forest just now, you said you were filling in for Father Pike, didn't you?"

"His sister was taken sick. He left last night."

Edwin nods, but there's something about this that rings utterly false. "Odd that I didn't hear anything about a boat going out last night, though."

"I have a confession to make," Roberts says.

"I'm listening."

"When I saw you in the forest, and I said I was going back to the church, well, I turned back for just a moment, as I was walking away."

Edwin stares at him. "What did you see?"

"I saw you walk under a maple tree. You were looking up, into the branches of the tree, and then—well, I had the impression that you could see something I couldn't. Was there something there?"

"I saw . . . well, I *thought* I saw—"

But Roberts is watching him too intensely, and in the quiet of this one-room church, at the far edge of the Western world, Edwin is oddly spooked. He's still a little ill—he has a pounding headache—and colossally weary. He doesn't want to talk anymore. He wants only to lie down. Roberts's presence here doesn't make sense to him.

"If Pike left last night," Edwin says, "he must have swum."

"But he did leave," Roberts says, "I assure you."

"Do you know how starved this place is for news, Father, really any news whatsoever? I live in the boardinghouse. If a boat had gone out last night, I would have heard about it at breakfast." The obvious next thought occurs to him: "Speaking of things I should have heard about, how did you get here? No boat's arrived in the past day or two, so am I to assume you strolled in through the forest?"

"Well," Roberts says, "I'm not sure how my mode of transportation is strictly relevant—"

Edwin rises, which forces Roberts to rise too. The priest backs into the aisle, and Edwin brushes past him.

"Edwin," Roberts says, but Edwin's already at the door. Another priest is approaching, climbing the stairs that lead up

from the road: Father Pike, just returning from a visit to the cannery or the logging camp, his shock of white hair all but shining
in the sunlight.

Edwin looks over his shoulder, into an empty church with its
back door hanging open. Roberts has fled.

Mirella and Vincent /

2020

1

"I'd like to show you something strange." The composer, who was famous in an extremely limited, niche kind of way, i.e., in zero danger of being recognized on the street but most people in a couple of smallish artistic subcultures knew his name, was obviously uncomfortable, sweating as he leaned in close to his mic. "My sister used to record videos. This next one is a video of hers that I found in storage, after her death, and it's got some kind of glitch in it that I can't explain." He was quiet for a moment, adjusting a knob on his keyboard. "I wrote some music to go with it, but right before the glitch, the music will go silent, so we can appreciate the beauty of technical imperfection."

The music began first, a dreamlike swelling of strings, suggestions of static just under the surface, and then the video: his sister had walked with her camera along a faint forest path, toward an old-growth maple tree. She stepped under the branches and angled her camera upward, into green leaves flashing in the sunlight, in the breeze, and the music stopped so abruptly that the silence seemed like the next beat. The beat after that was darkness: the screen went black, just for a second, and there was a brief confusion of overlapping sounds—a few notes of a violin, a dim cacophony like the interior of a metropolitan train station, a strange kind of *whoosh* that suggested hydraulic pressure— then in a heartbeat the moment was over, the tree was back, and there was some chaotic camerawork as the composer's sister seemingly looked around wildly, forgetting that she had the camera in her hand.

The composer's music resumed, that video shifting seamlessly into one of his newer works, this one involving a video that he'd shot himself, five or six minutes of an aggressively ugly street corner in Toronto, but with orchestral strings labouring to produce the idea of hidden beauty. The composer was working rapidly, playing sequences of notes on keyboards that emerged a beat later as violin music, building the music up in layers as the Toronto street corner ticked by on the screen over his head.

In the front row of the audience, Mirella Kessler was in tears. She'd been friends with the composer's sister—Vincent—and hadn't known that Vincent had died. She left the theatre soon after, and spent some time in the ladies' lounge, trying to pull herself together. Deep breaths, a fortifying layer of makeup. "Steady," she said aloud, to her face in the mirror. "Steady."

. . .

She'd come to this concert in the hope of speaking to the composer, in order to find out Vincent's whereabouts. There were certain questions she'd wanted to ask. Because in a version of her life so distant that it seemed now like a fairy tale, Mirella had had a husband—Faisal—and she and Faisal had been friends with Vincent and with Vincent's husband, Jonathan. There were several magnificent years, years of travel and money, and then the lights went out. Jonathan's investment fund turned out to be a Ponzi scheme. Faisal, unable to live in the face of financial ruin, took his own life.

Mirella had never spoken with Vincent again after that, because how could Vincent not have known? But a decade after Faisal's death she was at a restaurant with Louisa, her girlfriend of a year, and the first shiver of doubt crept in.

They were having dinner at a noodle place in Chelsea, and Louisa had been telling her about an unexpected birthday card from her Aunt Jacquie, whom Mirella had never met because at any given moment half of Louisa's family was feuding. "Jacquie's kind of awful most of the time," Louisa said, "but she came by it honestly, in my opinion."

"Why, what happened to her?"

"I never told you this story? It's epic. Her husband had a secret second family."

"Seriously? What a soap opera."

"It gets better." Louisa leaned forward to deliver the punch line: "He parked the second family *across the street*."

"What?"

"Yeah, it was amazing. Okay," Louisa said, "picture this scene. Hedge-fund guy, Park Avenue apartment, nonworking wife, two kids in private school. Peak Upper East Side. Then one day Aunt Jacquie checks the Amex statement, and there's a tuition payment to a private school that neither of her children attend. So she hands the statement to Uncle Mike, like, 'What's this crazy charge,' and apparently he almost has a heart attack on the spot."

"Go on."

"So my cousins, at the time they're in like eighth grade and ninth grade, something like that, but turns out Uncle Mike's also the father of the kindergartner across the street. He put the five-year-old's tuition payment on the wrong Amex."

"Wait, *literally* across the street?"

"Yeah, the buildings face each other. The doormen at both addresses probably knew for years."

"How could she not know?" Mirella asked, and just like that the past had swallowed her whole and she was talking about Vincent.

"A man who works long hours can hide anything," Louisa said. She was still talking about her aunt, and hadn't noticed that Mirella was elsewhere. "Lucky for you I don't work."

"Lucky for me," Mirella echoed, and kissed Louisa's hand. "What a crazy story."

"It's the across-the-street thing that gets me," Louisa said. "That geography was *brazen*."

"I can't decide if it's very lazy or very efficient." Mirella was pretending to still be there in the restaurant with Louisa, eating noodles, but she was far away. Vincent had sworn she hadn't known about her husband's crimes, in deleted voicemails and in a deposition.

"Mirella." Louisa's hand rested gently on Mirella's wrist. "Come back."

Mirella sighed, and set down her chopsticks.

"Did I ever tell you about my friend Vincent?"

"The wife of the Ponzi scheme guy?"

"Yeah. That story about your aunt made me think of her. Did I tell you I saw her once, after Faisal died?"

Louisa's eyes widened. "No."

"It was a little over a year after his death, so March or April of 2010. I went into a bar with some friends, and Vincent was the bartender."

"Oh my god. What did you say to her?"

"Nothing," Mirella said.

She hadn't recognized her at first. In the days of money, Vincent had had long wavy hair like all the other trophy wives, but in the bar her hair was cut very short, and she wore glasses and no makeup. In the moment the disguise had struck Mirella as vindication—*of* course *you're trying to hide, you monster*—but now a certain ambiguity had entered the scene: a reasonable alternate explanation for the short hair/glasses/no makeup was that one or another of her husband's defrauded investors could walk in at any moment. Manhattan was lousy with defrauded investors in those days.

"I pretended not to know her," she said now, to Louisa. "As revenge, I guess. It wasn't my best moment. She always said she didn't know what Jonathan had been doing, but I just thought, *Of course you knew. How could you possibly not have known. You knew and you let Faisal lose everything and now he's dead.* That was all I could think about in those days."

Louisa nodded. "Stands to reason that she'd know," she said.

"But what if she didn't?"

"Is it plausible that she didn't know?" Louisa asked.

"I didn't think so, at the time. But you're telling me this story about your poor Aunt Jacquie, and, well, if you can hide a five-year-old, you can hide a Ponzi scheme."

Louisa held Mirella's hands across the table. "You should talk to her."

"I have no idea how to find her."

"It's 2019," Louisa said. "No one's invisible."

But Vincent was. In those days Mirella was working as a receptionist at a high-end tile showroom near Union Square. It was the kind of place that required few customers, because when people spent money here, they spent tens of thousands of dollars. The morning after her dinner with Louisa, whiling away a silent hour behind a reception desk the size of a car, Mirella searched for Vincent. She tried Vincent's husband's surname first. A search for "Vincent Alkaitis" produced old society photos, some with Mirella in them—parties, galas, etc.—and also pages of Vincent at her husband's sentencing hearing, blank-faced, in a grey suit, and absolutely nothing else. The most recent images were from

2011. "Vincent Smith" turned up dozens of different people, mostly men, none of them the Vincent she was looking for. She couldn't find Vincent on social media, or anywhere else.

She leaned back in her chair, frustrated. High over her desk, a light was buzzing. Mirella wore a great deal of makeup at work, and when she was tired in the afternoons, sometimes her face felt heavy. Out on the white-tiled prairie of the sales floor, a lone sales rep was walking a customer through every conceivable colour of the company's signature composite material, which looked like stone but wasn't.

Vincent's parents were long dead, but she'd had a brother. Dredging up the brother's name required a deep dive into memory, which was a place Mirella generally tried to avoid. She glanced at the door to make sure no customers were approaching, then closed her eyes, took two deep breaths, and typed "Paul Smith + composer" into Google.

This was how she found herself at the Brooklyn Academy of Music four months later, waiting outside the stage door for Paul James Smith. She'd been hoping he could tell her how to find Vincent. But now Vincent was dead, apparently, which meant it was going to be a very different conversation. The stage door was on a quiet residential street. Mirella paced while she waited, not far, just a few feet in either direction. It was late January but unseasonably warm, well above freezing. Only one other person waited with her: a man of about her own age, mid-thirties, in jeans and a nondescript blazer. His clothes were too big. He nodded to her, she nodded back, and they settled into an awkward wait. Some time passed. A couple of staffers left without looking at them.

Then finally Vincent's brother emerged, looking a little haggard, although in fairness no one looked especially healthy in the orange glow of the streetlights here.

"Paul—" Mirella said, at the same moment that the other man said, "Excuse me—" and then they exchanged apologetic glances and fell silent, Paul glancing back and forth between them. A third man was approaching rapidly, a pale guy in a fedora and trench coat.

"Hello," Paul said, in a general way, to all of them.

"Hello!" said the newcomer. He took off his hat and revealed himself to be mostly bald. "Daniel McConaghy. Huge fan. Great show."

Paul gained an inch of height and a few watts of radiance as he stepped forward to shake the man's hand. "Well, thank you," he said, "always great to meet a fan." He looked around expectantly at Mirella and the guy in the oversized clothes.

"Gaspery Roberts," the oversized-clothes guy said. "Wonderful show."

"Hope you're not offended," the man in the fedora said, "I don't think your hands are dirty or anything, I've just gotten really into Purell since this thing in Wuhan hit the news." He was rubbing his hands together, with an apologetic smile.

"Fomites aren't a major mode of transmission with Covid-19," Gaspery said. *Fomites? Covid-19?* Mirella had never heard either term, and the other two were frowning too. "Oh,

right," Gaspery said, seemingly to himself, "it's only January."
He snapped back into focus. "Paul, could I maybe buy you a
drink and ask you a couple quick questions about your work?"
He had a faint accent that Mirella couldn't place.

"That sounds awesome," Paul said. "I could definitely use a
drink." He turned to Mirella.

"Mirella Kessler," she said. "I was friends with your sister."

"Vincent," he said quietly. She couldn't quite parse his expression. Sadness but also a flash of something furtive. For a moment
no one spoke. "Hey," he said, with forced cheer, "should we *all*
get a drink?"

They wound up at a little French restaurant a few blocks away,
across the street from a park that looked from Mirella's vantage
point like a hill barely contained by a high brick retaining wall.
She didn't know Brooklyn at all so everything was mysterious
here, no points of reference beyond a vague notion that if she
were to step outside the restaurant door, the spires of Manhattan would be somewhere to the left. The initial shock of the
news of Vincent's death had faded a little, replaced by a limit-
less exhaustion. She was sitting next to the guy in the fedora,
whose name she had forgotten, and across from Gaspery, who
sat next to Paul. The fedora was going on and on about Paul's
brilliance, his obvious influences, artistic debt to Warhol, etc.;
he'd loved Paul's work from the beginning, that groundbreaking
experimental collaboration with the video artist—what was his
name again?—at Miami Basel, what a leap it had been when

Paul suddenly started using his own videos instead of collaborating with others, and so on and so forth. Paul was glowing. He loved being praised, but who doesn't. She was facing the window, and her gaze kept drifting over Gaspery's shoulder to the park. If there were an earthquake and the retaining wall broke, would the park spill across the street and bury the restaurant? She returned her attention to the table when she heard Vincent's name.

"So your sister, Vincent, she's the one who filmed that strange video in your performance tonight?" This was Gaspery, his name memorable because she hadn't heard it before.

Paul laughed. "Name one of my videos that *isn't* strange," he said. "I did an interview last year, with this guy who kept calling me *sui generis,* and at a certain point I was like, 'Guy, you can just say *strange. Strange, weird,* or *eccentric,* take your pick.' Interview went a whole lot better after that, let me tell you." He laughed loudly at his own anecdote, and the fedora laughed too.

Gaspery smiled. "I meant that video with the forest path," he persisted. "With the darkness, the strange sounds."

"Oh. Yeah. That was Vincent's. She said I could use it."

"Was it filmed near where you grew up?" Gaspery asked.

"You've done your research," Paul said approvingly.

Gaspery inclined his head. "You're from British Columbia, aren't you?"

"Yeah. Tiny little place called Caiette, northern Vancouver Island."

"Oh, near Prince Edward Island," the fedora said confidently.

"Didn't really grow up there, though," Paul said, apparently not hearing this. "Vincent grew up there. Same dad, different moms, so I was just there summers and every second Christmas. But yeah, that's where the video was filmed."

"That . . . that moment in the video," Gaspery said, "that anomaly, for lack of a better word. Did you ever see anything like it in person?"

"Only on LSD," Paul said.

"Oh," the fedora said, brightening suddenly, "I didn't realize there was a psychedelic influence on your work." He leaned forward, in a confiding way. "I went pretty deep with psychedelics, myself. Once you get into heroic doses, you start to have certain realizations about the world. So much is an illusion, right?"

Gaspery shot him a troubled look. Mirella watched him while she waited for an opportunity to ask about Vincent. Gaspery seemed foreign in a way that she couldn't quite parse.

"And then once you grasp *that*," the fedora was saying, "it all just falls into place, right? Buddy of mine, he was struggling to quit cigarettes. Guy must've tried six or eight times. Not happening. Couldn't do it. Then one day he takes LSD, and *bam*. He calls me up the next evening, says, 'Dan, it's a miracle, I haven't even *wanted* a cigarette today.' I tell you, it was—"

"What happened to her?" Mirella asked Paul. She knew she was being rude but she didn't care, she was sitting there growing older by the minute, sinking into grief, and she wanted to know what had happened to her friend so she could leave these people.

Paul blinked at her, as if he'd forgotten she was there.

"She fell off a ship," he said. "About a year and a half—no, two years ago. It was two years last month."

"What kind of ship? Was she on a cruise?"

The fedora was glowering at his drink, but Gaspery was listening to the conversation with great interest.

"No, she was . . . I don't know how much you know about what happened to her in New York," Paul said, "that crazy thing with her husband, where it turned out he was a crook—"

"My husband was an investor in his Ponzi scheme," Mirella said. "I know all about it."

"Jesus," Paul said. "Did he—"

"Wait," the fedora said, "are we talking about Jonathan Alkaitis?"

"Yes," Paul said. "You know the story?"

"That crime was *insane,*" the fedora said. "What was the size of the fraud, twenty billion dollars? Thirty? I remember where I was when that story broke. Call comes in from my mom, turns out my dad's retirement savings were—"

"You were telling me about the boat," Mirella said.

Paul blinked. "Right. Yeah."

"You have a bit of an interrupting problem," the fedora said, to Mirella. "No offence."

"No one's talking to you," Mirella said. "I asked a question of Paul."

"Yeah, so Vincent and I, we were out of touch for a few years," Paul said, "but after Alkaitis abandoned her and fled the country,

I guess Vincent got some training and certifications and went to sea as a cook on a container ship."

"Oh," Mirella said. "Wow."

"Sounds like an interesting life, right?"

"What happened to her?"

"No one really knows," Paul said. "She just disappeared from the ship. Seems like it was an accident. No body."

Mirella didn't know she was going to cry until she felt tears spilling down her face. All of the men at the table looked acutely uncomfortable. Only Gaspery thought to pass her a napkin.

"She drowned," she said.

"Yeah. I mean, it seems like it. They were hundreds of miles from land. She disappeared in bad weather."

"Drowning was the thing she was most scared of." Mirella dabbed at her face with the napkin. In the quiet, the small noises of the restaurant swelled around them: a couple arguing softly in French at a nearby table, clattering from the kitchen, the restroom door closing.

"Well," Mirella said, "thanks for telling me. And thank you for the drink." She didn't know who was paying for the drink, but she knew it wasn't her. She rose and walked out of the restaurant without looking back.

Outside, she felt directionless. She knew she should get in an Uber and go home, just go home and sleep and not do anything stupid like go for a walk after dark in an unfamiliar borough, but Vincent was dead. She'd find somewhere to sit for a few minutes, Mirella decided, just to collect her thoughts. The neighbourhood seemed fairly tame to her and it wasn't that late, also she was afraid of nothing, so she crossed the street and entered the park.

The park was quiet, but by no means unoccupied. People moved through pools of light, couples with arms around one another's shoulders and small groups of friends, a woman singing to herself. She sensed free-floating menace in the air, but it wasn't directed toward her. How could Vincent be dead? It was impossible, everything about it. She found her way to a bench and put on her headphones so she could pretend not to hear if anyone spoke to her, and willed herself toward invisibility. She would sit here for a while, she would sit here and think about Vincent, or sit here until she could find a way to stop thinking about Vincent, then she would go home and go to bed. But her thoughts shifted toward Jonathan, Vincent's former husband, living out his life in a luxury hotel in Dubai. The thought of him being there, wherever he was, ordering room service and asking to have the sheets changed and swimming in the hotel pool—*while Vincent was dead*—was an abomination.

A man walked in front of her and sat on the bench. She turned and it was Gaspery, so she took off the headphones.

"Forgive me," he said, "I saw you go into the park, and it's not a bad neighbourhood, but—" He didn't finish the thought, because he didn't have to. For a woman alone in a park after nightfall, every neighbourhood is a bad neighbourhood.

"Who are you?" Mirella asked.

"I'm a kind of investigator," Gaspery said. "You'll think I'm crazy if I get into the details."

There was something familiar about him, it seemed to her now, something about his profile that rang a distant bell, but she couldn't quite place him.

"What are you investigating?"

"Look, I'll be frank with you, I have no interest in Mr. Smith or his art," Gaspery said.

"That makes two of us."

"But I'm interested in, well, in a certain kind of anomaly, like that moment in the video when the screen goes black. I waited outside the stage door to ask him about it."

"It is a strange moment."

"Can I ask, did your friend ever talk about that moment? Since it was her video, after all."

"No," Mirella said, "not that I remember."

"Stands to reason," Gaspery said. "She would've been quite young when she shot that video. The things we see when we're young, sometimes they don't stay with us."

The things we see when we're young.

"I think I've seen you before," Mirella said. She was looking at his face in profile in the dim light. He turned to look at her, and she was certain of it. "In Ohio."

"You look like you've seen a ghost."

She rose from the bench. "You were under the overpass," she said. "In Ohio, when I was a kid. That was you, wasn't it?"

He frowned. "I think you're mistaking me for someone."

"No, I think it was you. You were under the overpass. Right before the police came, before you were arrested. You said my name."

But he looked genuinely confused. "Mirella, I—"

"I have to go." She fled, not quite running, but walking in the flying unstoppable way that she'd perfected over years in New York City, darting out of the park, back down to the street, where in the fishbowl glow of the French restaurant the fedora and Vincent's brother were still deep in conversation. Gaspery hadn't followed her. She was grateful that he was wearing a white shirt; he would all but shine in the dark. She plunged into the shadows of a residential street. She flew past old brownstones standing beautiful in the streetlights, iron fences, old trees; faster and faster, toward the bright lights of a commercial avenue up ahead, where a yellow cab was gliding across the intersection like a chariot, like some kind of miracle—a yellow cab in Brooklyn!— and she hailed it and climbed aboard. A moment later the taxi was speeding over the Brooklyn Bridge, Mirella crying quietly in the backseat. The driver glanced at her in the rearview mirror, but—oh, the grace of strangers in this crowded city!—said nothing.

2

When Mirella was a child, she lived with her mother and her older sister, Susanna, in a duplex in exurban Ohio. The housing development was located in a territory composed of strip malls and big-box stores. Farmland extended to the back of the Walmart parking lot. Some miles away, there was a prison. Mirella's mother worked two jobs and spent very little time at home. In the early mornings—well before dawn in the wintertime—Mirella and Susanna's mother rose after a few hours of sleep, poured milk over her daughters' cereal and did their hair while blearily drinking coffee, and drove them to school. She kissed her daughters goodbye and they were at school for the next ten hours—early drop-off, then school, then after-school programming—until at the end of the afternoon they boarded a bus that dropped them a half-mile from home.

It was a bad half-mile. They had to walk under an overpass.

The overpass scared Mirella, but in all the years she lived there, from when she was five until she dropped out of school and took a bus to New York City at sixteen, there was only one truly terrible incident. Mirella was nine, which made Susanna eleven, and they did hear the gunshots as the school bus pulled away, but the sounds were clear only in retrospect. In the moment, they looked at each other in the winter twilight and Susanna shrugged. "Probably just a car backfiring or something," she said, and Mirella, who would have believed anything Susanna told her, took her sister's hand and they walked together. Snow was falling. The mouth of the overpass was a dark cave waiting to swallow them. *It's fine*, Mirella told herself, *it's fine, it's fine*, because it was always fine, but this particular time it wasn't. As they stepped into the shadows, the sound came once more, impossibly loud now. They stopped.

Two men lay on the ground a few yards ahead of them. One was perfectly still; the other was twitching. In the dim light, at this distance, she couldn't see exactly what had happened to them. A third man was sitting slumped against the wall, a handgun dangling loose in his hand. A fourth was running away—his footsteps echoed—but Mirella glimpsed him for only an instant, scrambling up the embankment at the far end of the overpass and out of sight.

For a long time all of them—Mirella, Susanna, the man with the gun, the two dead or dying men on the ground—were frozen in a winter tableau. How much time? It felt like forever. Hours, days. The man with the gun had a sleepy, sedated look about him; his head nodded forward once or twice. Then came the police lights, blue and red washing over him, and this seemed to wake him up. He stared at the gun in his hand, as if unsure how it had arrived there, then he turned his head, and looked directly at the girls.

"Mirella," he said.

Then came shouting and confusion, a swarm of dark uniforms—"*Drop your weapon! Drop your weapon!*"—and although the event objectively happened, she and Susanna really were interviewed by the police, and there really was a story in the papers the next day ("Two Shot Dead Under Overpass: Suspect in Custody"), it was easy to convince herself in the years that followed that she'd only imagined this last part, that he hadn't really said her name. How could he have known her name? Susanna didn't remember hearing anything.

But all these years later, in the back of a Manhattan-bound taxi, safe in another life, here was a certainty she couldn't shake: the man in the tunnel was Gaspery Roberts.

She closed her eyes, trying to relax, but her phone vibrated in her hand. A text from her girlfriend: *Are you coming to Jess's party?*

It took a moment to remember. She texted back—*On my way*—and waved to catch the driver's eye in the rearview mirror.

"Excuse me."

"Ma'am?" he said, a little wary because she'd just been crying.

"May I give you a new destination? I need to get to Soho."

3

She had to walk all the way through the party before she found Louisa, smoking a cigarette on a terrace that was really just a tiny patch of blacktop roof. She kissed her and then sat awkwardly beside her on a narrow stone bench.

"How are you doing?" Louisa asked. They lived separately but spent a great deal of time together.

"Not bad at all," Mirella said, because she didn't want to talk about it. It was troublingly easy to lie to Louisa. She knew it was unfair to compare people, everyone knows that, but a difficulty she was having at this moment was that Louisa seemed infinitely less interesting to her than Vincent. Louisa had a kind of unspoiled quality, an air of having been cushioned from life's sharper edges, which was less appealing now than it had been. "I'm a little tired," Mirella said. "I didn't sleep that well."

"How come?"

"I don't know, just one of those random bad nights."

Another difficulty of the evening: this was Jess's party, and Jess was Mirella's friend, not Louisa's. In Mirella's old life, her long-ago life wherein everything was different, she'd been to this terrace with Faisal. Now, as then, the space was dressed up with fairy lights and potted palms, but still felt a little like the bottom of a hole. This was the downside to having retained a few friends from her time with Faisal—there were dangerous places here and there, places where she could get sucked into memories of another life, and this terrace was among them. On another night, at another party—fourteen years ago? thirteen?—she and Vincent had stood out here, a little drunk, looking straight up at the tiny patch of dark sky because Vincent swore she could see the North Star.

"It's right there," Vincent said. "Look, follow my finger. It's not that bright."

"That's a satellite," Mirella said.

"*What's* a satellite?" Faisal asked, stepping out onto the balcony. They'd arrived separately, and this was the first time she'd seen him all day. She kissed him and didn't quite fail to see the way Vincent glanced in their direction before returning her gaze to the sky. A difference between Mirella and Vincent was that Mirella truly loved her husband.

"There," Mirella said, pointing. "It's moving, right?"

Faisal squinted. "I'll have to take your word for it," he said.

"I think I need new glasses." He glanced around the cramped space, his arm around her waist. "Wow," he said, "what a thrillingly boho firetrap."

It was true. Buildings rose up on all sides. Three walls belonged to other buildings, and the fourth held the door that led back into the party. All these years later, sitting out here with Louisa, Mirella closed her eyes momentarily in order to not see Faisal gazing up at the sky.

"What did you do all day?" Louisa asked.

There had been a time when Mirella liked Louisa's questions—what a gift, she'd once thought, to be with someone who was so *interested,* interested in everything she'd done all day, someone who cared enough to ask—but tonight it was an intrusion.

"Went for a walk. Did some laundry. Stared at Instagram, mostly." Gaspery Roberts couldn't possibly have been the man under the overpass, now that she thought about it, because that was decades ago and he hadn't aged.

"Was that satisfying?"

"Of course not," Mirella said, a little sharper than she'd intended, and Louisa gave her a surprised look.

"We should go somewhere," Louisa said. "Maybe rent a cottage, get out of the city for a few days."

"That sounds nice." But Mirella was startled by the unhappiness that flooded through her at the suggestion. She very much did not want to go to a cottage with Louisa, she realized.

"But first," Louisa said, "I need another drink." She went inside and Mirella was alone for a while, then a woman came over to ask for a light and offered to tell Mirella's fortune in return. Mirella held her hands out as instructed, palms up, embarrassed by the way they trembled. How could she have fallen out of love with Louisa so suddenly, so cleanly? How could the man in the tunnel in Ohio have surfaced all these years later in New York? How could Vincent be dead? The fortune-teller put her hands over Mirella's hands, their palms almost touching, and closed her eyes. Mirella liked being able to watch her unobserved. The fortune-teller was older than Mirella had thought at first, somewhere in her thirties, first lines visible on her face. She was wearing a complicated arrangement of scarves.

"Where are you from?" she asked.

"Ohio."

"No, I mean originally."

"Still Ohio."

"Oh. I thought maybe I heard an accent."

"The accent's from Ohio too."

The fortune-teller's eyes were still closed.

"You have a secret," she said.

"Doesn't everyone?"

Her eyes opened. "You tell me yours, I'll tell you mine, and we'll never see each other again," she said.

It was an attractive proposition. "Okay," Mirella said. "But you go first."

"My secret is, I hate people," the woman said, very sincerely, and for the first time Mirella liked her.

"All people?"

"All except maybe like three," she said. "Your turn."

"My secret is, I want to kill a man." Was this true? Mirella wasn't sure. It had a ring of truth about it.

The fortune-teller's eyes darted over Mirella's face, like she was trying to work out if this was some kind of joke. "A specific man?" she asked. She smiled tentatively—*You're kidding, right? Please tell me you're kidding?*—but Mirella didn't smile back.

"Yes," Mirella said. "A specific man." It became real as she said it.

"What's his name?"

"Jonathan Alkaitis." When had she last said the name out loud? She repeated it to herself, more quietly this time. "Actually, maybe I just want to talk to him. I don't know."

"Pretty big difference," the fortune-teller said.

"Yeah." Mirella closed her eyes against the dark of the sky, the tumult of the nearby party, the reek of cigarette smoke, the fortune-teller's face. "I guess I'll have to make up my mind."

"Okay," the fortune-teller said, "well, thanks for the light." She slid away from Mirella and vanished into the party, through an open door like a portal into a lost world. It was a cold night, and the moon was brilliant over New York City. Mirella stood looking at it for a moment, then returned to the party, which felt like a dream she'd had once, all abstract colour and commotion and lights. Louisa was dancing in the living room. Mirella stood watching her for a moment, then waded through the crowd.

"I've got a headache," Mirella said. "I think I'm going to go."

Louisa kissed her, and Mirella knew it was over. She felt nothing. "Call me," Louisa said.

"Adieu," Mirella said as she backed away through the crowd, and Louisa, who spoke no French and didn't understand the implication, blew her a kiss.

3

Last Book Tour on Earth /

2203

THE FIRST STOP ON THE BOOK TOUR WAS NEW YORK CITY, where Olive did signing events at two bookstores and then found an hour to walk in Central Park before the bookseller dinner. The Sheep Meadow at twilight: silvery light, wet leaves on the grass. The sky was crowded with low-altitude airships, and in the distance the falling-star lights of commuter aircraft streaked upward toward the colonies. Olive paused for a moment to orient herself, then walked toward the ancient double silhouette of the Dakota. Hundred-story towers rose up behind it.

The Dakota was where Olive's new publicist, Aretta, was waiting, in charge of all events in the Atlantic Republic. Aretta was a little younger than Olive, and deferential in a way that made Olive nervous. When Olive walked into the lobby, Aretta stood quickly, and the hologram with whom she'd been speaking blinked out. "Did you have a nice walk in the park?" she asked, already smiling in anticipation of a positive reply.

"It was lovely, thank you," Olive said. She didn't add *It made me wish I could live on Earth,* because the last time she'd confided in a handler, it was repeated at dinner—"Do you know what Olive told me on the ride over?" a librarian in Montreal had reported breathlessly to a restaurant table full of waiting librarians, "She told me she was a little nervous before her talk!"—

so now as a matter of policy Olive didn't reveal anything even remotely personal to anyone ever.

"Well," Aretta said, "we should probably be getting to the venue. It's about six or seven blocks, should we maybe just . . . ?"

"I'd love to walk," Olive said, "if you don't mind." They walked out together into the silver city.

Did Olive actually wish she could live on Earth? She vacillated on the question. She'd lived all her life in the hundred and fifty square kilometres of the second moon colony, the imaginatively named Colony Two. She found it beautiful—Colony Two was a city of white stone, spired towers, tree-lined streets and small parks, alternating neighbourhoods of tall buildings and little houses with miniature lawns, a river running under pedestrian archways—but there's something to be said for unplanned cities. Colony Two was soothing in its symmetry and its order. Sometimes order can be relentless.

In the signing line after the lecture in Manhattan that night, a young man knelt on his side of the table so that he was more or less at eye level with Olive, and said, "I have a book to sign"— his voice trembled a little—"but what I really wanted to tell you is that your work helped me through a bad patch last year. I'm grateful."

"Oh," Olive said. "Thank you. I'm honoured." But in these moments *honoured* always felt inadequate, which made it feel

like the wrong word, which made Olive feel somehow fraudu-
lent, like an actor playing the role of Olive Llewellyn.

"Everyone feels like a fraud sometimes," Dad said the following
day, on the drive from the Denver airship terminal to the tiny
town where he lived with Olive's mother.

"Oh, I know," Olive said. "I'm not suggesting it's an actual
problem." Olive's understanding of her own life was that she
didn't have any actual problems.

"Right." Dad smiled. "I'd imagine your life's a little disorienting these days."

"Perhaps just a little." Olive had forty-eight hours to see her
parents before the tour resumed. They were passing through
an agricultural zone, enormous robots moving slowly over the
fields. The sunlight here was sharper than at home. "I'm grateful
for all of it," she said. "Disorienting or not."

"Sure. Must be hard to be away from Sylvie and Dion, though."

Now they were in the outskirts of the little town where her
parents lived, passing through a district of robot repair foundries.

"I just try not to think about it," Olive said. The grey of the
foundries was subsiding into brightly painted little shops and
houses. The clock in the town square glinted in the sunlight.

"The distance is unbearable if you let yourself dwell on it."
Her father's gaze was fixed on the road. "Here we are," he said.
They were turning onto her parents' street, and there, so close,
her mother stood in the doorway. Olive leaped down from the

hovercraft the moment it stopped, and ran into her mother's arms. *If the distance is unbearable,* she didn't ask, then or in the two days she stayed with her parents, *then why do you live so far from me?*

Olive's parents' house couldn't be called her childhood home—her childhood home had been sold a few weeks after she left for college, when her parents decided to retire on Earth—but there was peace here. "It was so good to see you," her mother whispered when she left. She held Olive for just a moment, and stroked her hair. "Come back soon?"

A hovercraft was waiting outside the house, the driver hired by one of Olive's North American publishers. She had an event at a bookstore in Colorado Springs that night, followed by an early-morning flight to a festival in Deseret.

"I'll bring Sylvie and Dion next time," Olive said, and stepped back into the tour.

A book tour paradox: Olive missed her husband and daughter with a desperate passion, but also she liked very much being alone in the empty streets of Salt Lake City at eight-thirty in the morning on a Saturday in the bright autumn air, birds wheeling in white light. There's something to be said for looking up at a clear blue sky and knowing that it isn't a dome.

In the Republic of Texas the next afternoon, she wanted to go for a walk again, because on the map, her hotel—a La Quinta that faced another La Quinta, a parking lot between them—was just across the road from a cluster of restaurants and shops, but what the map didn't show was that the road was an eight-lane expressway with no crosswalk and constant traffic, mostly modern hovercraft but also the occasional defiantly retro wheeled pickup truck, so she walked along the expressway for a while with the shops and the restaurants shining like a mirage on the other side. There was no way to cross without risking her life, so she didn't. When she got back to her hotel she felt something scratching her ankles, and when she looked down her socks were spiked with little burrs, astonishingly sharp black-brown stars like miniature weapons that had to be extracted very carefully. She set them on the desk and photographed them from every angle. They were so perfectly hard and shiny that they could've passed for biotech, but when she pulled one apart, she saw that it was real. No, *real* wasn't the word for it. Everything that can be touched is real. What she saw was it was a thing that grew, a castoff from some mysterious plant they didn't have in the moon colonies, so she wrapped a few of them in a sock and carefully stowed the sock away in her suitcase to give to her daughter, Sylvie, who was five and collected that kind of thing.

"I was so confused by your book," a woman in Dallas said. "There were all these strands, narratively speaking, all these characters, and I felt like I was waiting for them to connect, but they didn't, ultimately. The book just ended. I was like"—she was some distance away, in the darkened audience, but Olive saw that she was miming flipping through a book and running out of pages—"I was just like, *Huh? Is the book missing pages? It just ended.*"

"Okay," Olive said. "So just to clarify, your question is . . ."

"I was just, like, *what*," the woman said. "My question is just . . ." She spread her hands, like *help me out here, I've run out of words.*

The hotel room that night was all black and white. Olive had dreams about playing chess with her mother.

Did the book end too abruptly? She fixated on the question for three days, from the Republic of Texas to western Canada.

"I'm trying not to be pessimistic," Olive said, on the phone to her husband, "but I've barely slept in three days and I doubt I'll be terribly impressive in my lecture tonight." This was in Red Deer. Outside the hotel room window, the lights of residential towers glimmered in the dark.

"Don't be pessimistic," Dion said. "Think of that quote I've got pinned up in my office."

" 'It's a great life if you don't weaken,' " Olive said. "How's work going, speaking of your office?"

He sighed. "I got assigned to the new project." Dion was an architect.

"The new university?"

"Yeah, kind of. A centre for the study of physics, but also . . .

I signed an ironclad confidentiality agreement, so don't tell anyone?"

"Of course. I won't tell a soul. But what's so secret about the architecture of a university?"

"It's not quite . . . I'm not sure it's exactly a university." Dion sounded troubled. "There's some serious weirdness in the blue-prints."

"What kind of weirdness?"

"Well, for starters, there's a tunnel under the street connecting the building to Security Headquarters," he said.

"Why would a university need a tunnel to the police?"

"Your guess is as good as mine. And the building backs up on the government building," Dion said, "which, I mean, at first I thought nothing of it. That's prime downtown real estate, so you know, why shouldn't the university build next to the government building, but the two buildings aren't separate. There are so many passageways between them that it's functionally the same building."

"You're right," Olive said, "that seems weird."

"Well, it's a good project for my portfolio, I guess."

Olive understood from his tone that he wanted to change the subject. "How's Sylvie?"

"Doing fine." Dion immediately pivoted the conversation to some trivial matter involving the grocery order and Sylvie's school lunches, from which she understood that Sylvie probably wasn't in fact doing particularly well in her absence, and she was grateful for his kindness in not telling her this.

. . .

In the morning she flew to a city in the far north for a day of interviews, and then she had an evening lecture, and then there was a long signing line and a late dinner, followed by three hours of sleep and a three-forty-five a.m. airport pickup.

"What do you do, Olive?" the driver asked.

"I'm a writer," Olive said. She closed her eyes and rested her head against the window, but the driver spoke again:

"What do you write?"

"Books."

"Tell me more."

"Well," Olive said, "I'm travelling because of a novel called *Marienbad*. It's about a pandemic."

"That's your most recent?"

"No, I've written two others since then. But *Marienbad*'s being made into a film, so I'm on tour for a new edition."

"That's so interesting," the driver said, and started talking about a book she wanted to write. It seemed to be some kind of sci-fi/fantasy epic, the modern world except with wizards, demons, and talking rats. The rats were good. They helped the wizards. They were rats because in all the books the driver had read that involved helpful talking animals, the animals were just too big. Horses and dragons and whatnot. But how do you discreetly move through the world with a dragon or a horse? It's untenable. Try taking a horse into a bar sometime. No, what you want, she said, is a pocket-sized animal sidekick, a rat for example.

"Yeah, I guess rats are more portable," Olive said. She was trying to keep her eyes open, but it was very difficult. The massive transport truck in front of them kept weaving over the centre line. Human-driven, or a flaw in the software? Unsettling either way. The driver was talking about the possibilities of the multiverse: rats can't talk here, she pointed out, but does it logically follow that they can't talk *anywhere*? She seemed to be waiting for a reply.

"Well, I don't know much about rat anatomy," Olive said, "like if their voice boxes and vocal cords or whatever are up to the task of human speech, but I'll have to think about it, maybe rats in different universes could have different anatomy . . ." (She may have been mumbling by that point, or possibly not speaking at all. It was so hard to stay awake.) The back of the transport truck was beautiful, a diamond-patterned textured steel that glinted and shone in the headlights.

"I mean, for all we know," the driver was saying, "there's a universe where your book is real, I mean nonfictional!"

"I hope not," Olive said. She could only keep her eyes halfopen, so the lights in her field of vision were streaked into vertical spikes, the dashboard, the tail lights, the reflections off the back of the truck.

"So your book," the driver said, "it's about a pandemic?"

"Yes. A scientifically implausible flu." Olive couldn't keep her eyes open anymore, so she surrendered, she closed her eyes and let herself fall into the kind of half-sleep from which she knew she could be summoned by a voice—

"Have you been following the news about this new thing," the driver said, "this new virus in Australia?"

"Kind of," Olive said, with her eyes closed. "It seems like it's been fairly well contained."

"You know, in my book," the driver said, "there's a kind of apocalypse too." She talked for some time about a catastrophic rip in the space-time continuum, but Olive was too tired to follow.

"I've kept you up this whole time!" the driver said brightly, as the car pulled into the airport. "You didn't get to sleep at all!"

Twelve hours later, Olive was delivering her *Marienbad* lecture, which leaned heavily on her research into the history of pandemics. The lecture was so familiar at this point that it required very little in the way of conscious thought, and her mind was wandering. She kept thinking about the conversation with the driver, because she remembered saying *It seems like it's been fairly well contained,* but here's an epidemiological question: If you're talking about outbreaks of infectious disease, isn't *fairly well contained* essentially the same thing as *not contained at all*? *Focus,* she told herself, and pulled herself back to the reality of the podium, the hard bright light, the microphone.

"In the spring of 1792," she said, "Captain George Vancouver sailed northward up the coast of what would later become British Columbia, aboard the HMS *Discovery*. As he and his crew travelled northward, the men found themselves increasingly unsettled. Here was this temperate climate, this incredibly green landscape, and yet it seemed strangely empty. Vancouver wrote in his shipboard diary: 'We travelled nearly one hundred fifty miles of those shores, without seeing that number of inhabitants.' " A pause to let that sink in, while Olive took a sip of water. A virus is either contained or it isn't. It's a binary condition. She hadn't been sleeping enough. She set down her water glass.

"When they ventured ashore, they found villages that could have housed hundreds, but those villages were abandoned. When they ventured farther, they realized that the forest was a grave-yard." This was the part of the lecture that had been easy before giving birth to her daughter, and was now almost impossible. Olive paused to steady herself. "Canoes with human remains were strung three or four metres up in the trees," she said. *Human remains that were not Sylvie. Not Sylvie. Not Sylvie.* "Elsewhere, they found skeletons on the beach. Because small-pox had already arrived."

In the signing line after that night's lecture, signing her name over and over again, Olive's thoughts kept drifting toward disaster. *To Xander with best wishes Olive Llewellyn. To Claudio with best wishes Olive Llewellyn. To Sohail with best wishes Olive Llewellyn. To Hyeseung with best wishes Olive Llewellyn.* Was there going to be another pandemic? A new cluster of cases had appeared in New Zealand that morning.

The hotel room that night was mostly beige, with a painting of some extravagantly petalled pink Earth flower—a peony?—over the bed.

. . .

"A year earlier," Olive told another crowd, same lecture/different city, "in 1791, a trading ship, the *Columbia Rediviva*, had sailed those same waters. They were trading sea otter skins." What did a sea otter even look like? Olive had never seen one. She resolved to look this up later. "They had a similar experience. They found a depopulated land, and the very few survivors they encountered had terrible stories and terrible scars. ' 'Twas evident that these Natives had been visited by that scourge of mankind the smallpox,' wrote a crew member, John Boit. Another sailor, John Hoskins, was moved to outrage: 'Infamous Europeans, a scandal to the Christian name; is it you,' he wrote, 'who bring and leave in a country with people you deem savages the most loathsome diseases?' "

A sip of water. The audience was silent. (A passing thought that felt like triumph: *I am holding the room*.) "But of course," she said, "there's always a beginning. Before smallpox could be brought from Europe to the Americas, smallpox had to arrive in Europe."

She got out of bed that night and walked into a side table, because she'd been thinking about the layout of the previous night's hotel room.

The next morning, on a long drive between cities, the driver asked if Olive had kids back home.

"I have a daughter," Olive said.

"How old?"

"Five."

"What are you doing here, then?" the driver asked.

"Well, this is how I provide for her," she said, in her mildest voice, and didn't add *Fuck you, I know you would never ask a man that question,* because after all it was just the two of them alone in the car, this man and Olive. Watching the trees slip by outside the window; they were passing through a forest preserve. Imagining Sylvie was here beside her, imagining that if she wanted to she could reach out and hold that warm little hand.

"You grew up there? In the colonies?" he asked abruptly, after some time had passed. They'd been talking about the moon colonies earlier.

"Yes. My grandmother was one of the first settlers."

She liked to picture her grandmother sometimes, twenty years old, rising out of the Vancouver Airship Terminal in the first light of dawn, her ship streaking out into the dark.

"Always meant to go up there," the driver said. "Never made it."

Remember that you're lucky to get to travel. Remember that some people never leave this planet. Olive closed her eyes, in order to better imagine that Sylvie was sitting beside her.

"You smell nice, by the way," the driver said.

The next four hotel rooms were white and grey and had identical layouts, because all four hotels were part of the same chain.

"Is this your first time staying with us?" a woman at a reception desk for the third or fourth hotel said to her, and Olive wasn't sure how to answer, because if you've stayed in one Marriott, haven't you stayed in all of them?

Another city:

"Before smallpox could be brought from Europe to the Americas, smallpox had to arrive in Europe." Olive was regretting her decision to wear a sweater. The lights in Toronto were too hot. "In the middle of the second century, Roman soldiers returning from their siege of the Mesopotamian city of Seleucia brought a new illness back to the capital.

"Victims of the Antonine Plague, as it came to be called, developed fevers, vomiting, and diarrhea. A few days later, a terrible rash would appear on their skin. The population had no immunity." Olive had delivered the lecture so many times that she felt at this point like a neutral observer. She listened to the words and cadences from some distance away.

"When the Antonine Plague raged through the Roman Empire," Olive told the audience, "the army was decimated. There were parts of the empire where one in three people died. Here's something interesting: the Romans wondered if they'd brought this calamity upon themselves, by their actions in the city of Seleucia."

She was in that night's hotel room—mostly beige and blue, with pink accents—when Dion called. This was unusual: generally speaking, she called him. Dion sounded tired. He'd been working long hours, he said, and the new university project was creepy, and Sylvie was being difficult. When he'd picked Sylvie up at school today she hadn't wanted to leave and had made a scene and everyone had felt sorry for him, he could see it in their soft expressions. "Have you been following the news about this new illness in Australia?" he asked. "I'm kind of worried about it."

"Not really," Olive said. "To be honest, I've been too tired to think."

"I wish you could come home."

"I'll be home soon."

He was silent.

"I should go," she said. "Good night."

"Good night," he said, and hung up.

"In the city of Seleucia," Olive told a crowd at the Mercantile Library in Cincinnati, a day or two later, "the Roman army had destroyed the temple of Apollo. In that temple, the historian Ammianus Marcellinus wrote, Roman soldiers had discovered a narrow crevice. When the Romans opened this hole wider, in the hope that it might contain valuables, Marcellinus wrote that there 'issued a pestilence, loaded with the force of incurable disease, which . . . polluted the whole world from the borders of Persia to the Rhine and Gaul with contagion and death.'"

A beat. A sip of water. Pacing is everything.

"This explanation might seem a little silly to us now, but they were grasping wildly for an explanation for the nightmare that had befallen them, and I think that in its outlandishness, the explanation touches upon the root of our fear: illness still carries a terrible mystery."

She looked over the crowd and saw, as always at this point in the lecture, that particular look on the faces of some of the audience, a specific grief. In any given crowd, several people will inevitably be incurably sick, and several others will have recently lost someone they love to illness.

"Are you worried about the new virus?" Olive asked the library director in Cincinnati. They were sitting together in the director's office, which Olive had immediately ranked as possibly her favourite of all the offices she'd ever seen. It was located beneath the stacks, which were hundreds of years old and made of wrought iron.

"I'm trying not to be," the director said. "I'm hoping it'll just fizzle out."

"I suppose they usually do," Olive said. Was this true? She was unsure as she spoke.

The library director nodded, her eyes wandering. She clearly didn't want to talk about pandemics. "Let me tell you something magnificent about this place," she said.

"Oh, please do," Olive said. "It's been a while since anyone's told me anything magnificent."

"So we don't own the building," the director said, "but we hold a ten-thousand-year lease on the space."

"You're right. That's magnificent."

"Nineteenth-century hubris. Imagine thinking civilization

would still exist in ten thousand years. But there's more." She leaned forward, paused for effect. "The lease is renewable."

The window in that night's hotel room opened, which after a dozen rooms with nonopening windows felt like something of a miracle. Olive spent a long time reading a novel by the window, in the beautiful fresh air.

The next morning, leaving Cincinnati, Olive saw a sunrise from the airport lounge. Heat shimmering over the tarmac, the horizon cast in pink. *Paradox: I want to go home but I could watch Earth's sunrises forever.*

"The truth is," Olive said, behind a lectern in Paris, "even now, all these centuries later, for all our technological advances, all our scientific knowledge of illness, we still don't always know why one person gets sick and another doesn't, or why one patient survives and another dies. Illness frightens us because it's chaotic. There's an awful randomness about it."

At the reception that night, someone tapped her shoulder, and when she turned around it was Aretta, her publicist from the Atlantic Republic.

"Aretta!" she said. "What are you doing in Paris?"

"I'm off work," Aretta said, "but one of my best friends works for your French publisher and she got us tickets for the reception, so I thought I'd say hi."

"It's good to see you here," Olive said, and meant it, but someone was pulling her away to speak to a group of sponsors and booksellers, so for a while afterward Olive stood in a circle of people who wanted to know when her next book was coming out and whether she was enjoying France and where her family was.

"You must have a very kind husband," a woman said, "to look after your daughter while you do this."

"What do you mean?" Olive asked, but of course she knew what the woman meant.

"Well, he's looking after your daughter, while you do this," the woman said.

"Forgive me," Olive said, "I fear there's a problem with my translator bot. I thought you said he was kind to care for his own child." As she turned away, she realized that she was grinding her teeth. She looked for Aretta but couldn't find her.

The next four hotel rooms were beige, blue, beige again, then mostly white, but all four had silk flowers in a vase on the desk.

"What's it like?" the interviewer asked. It was difficult to stop thinking about the woman in Paris, but Olive was trying. *Keep moving.* Olive and the interviewer were onstage in Tallinn. The lights were very hot.

"What do you mean?" It was a strange opening question.

"What's it like writing such a successful book? What's it like being Olive Llewellyn?"

"Oh. It's surreal, actually. I wrote three books that no one noticed, no distribution beyond the moon colonies, and then . . . it's like slipping into a parallel universe," Olive said. "When I published *Marienbad,* I somehow fell into a bizarre upside-down world where people actually read my work. It's extraordinary. I hope I never get used to it."

The driver who took Olive to her hotel that night had a beautiful voice and sang an old jazz song as he drove. Olive opened the hovercraft window and closed her eyes in order to live more completely in the music, cool air in her face, and for several minutes she was perfectly happy.

"It's amazing how time slows when I'm travelling," Olive said, on the phone to Dion. She was lying on her back on the floor of another hotel room, staring up at the ceiling. The bed would have been more comfortable, but her back hurt and the hard floor was helping. "I feel like I've been on the road for six months. I'm not sure how it's still November."

"It's been three weeks."

"Like I said."

There was silence on the line.

"Look," Olive said, "the thing is, it's possible to be grateful for extraordinary circumstances and simultaneously long to be with the people you love."

She felt a softening between them before he spoke. "I know, love," Dion said gently. "We miss you too."

"I've been thinking about your project," she said. "Why a

university would need an underground passageway to police headquarters and—"

But Dion's device was ringing. "I'm sorry," he said, "it's my boss. Talk soon?"

"Talk soon."

She'd been on an airship crossing the Atlantic when the answer to the puzzle came to her.

Research teams had been working on time travel for decades, both on Earth and in the colonies. In that context, a university for the study of physics with an underground passageway to the police headquarters and countless literal back doors into government made perfect sense. What is time travel if not a security problem?

She kept searching for the song the driver in Tallinn had been singing, but she couldn't find it. The lyrics evaded her. She kept entering search terms into her device (*love + rain + death + money + lyrics + song*) and getting nowhere.

In Lyon, at a festival dedicated to mystery fiction, Olive's French publicist brought her to a media room where the interviewer, a woman who worked for a magazine, was programming an array of hologram cameras. "Olive," the interviewer said, "I love your work."

"Thank you, that's really nice to hear."

"Will you sit in that chair, please?"

Olive sat. An assistant affixed a mic to her shirt.

"So this is a feature I'm doing with all of the authors at the festival," the interviewer said, "just a brief interview feature. It's a fun thing for our audience."

"A fun thing?" Olive was troubled. Her French publicist shot the interviewer a look of alarm.

"Shall we get started?"

"Sure." Ten holographic cameras floated through the air and surrounded Olive like a ring of stars, building their composite impression.

"So these questions," the interviewer said, "they have a mystery focus!"

"Because we're at a mystery festival," Olive said.

"Exactly. Okay. Number one: What's your favourite alibi?"

"My favourite . . . alibi?"

"Yes."

"I don't really . . . I just say I have other plans. When I don't want to do something."

"I understand you're married to a man," the interviewer said. "When you met your husband, what was your first clue that you loved him?"

"Well," Olive said, "I guess just a sense of recognition, if that makes sense. I remember the first time I saw him, I looked at him and I knew he'd be important in my life. Is that a clue, though?"

"What's your idea of the perfect murder?"

"I remember reading a story once where a guy got stabbed with an icicle," Olive said. "I guess that's sort of perfect, a crime where the murder weapon melts. Do you mind if I ask, though, do you have any questions that have to do with my work?"

"I just have one more. Okay, last question. Sex with or without handcuffs?"

Olive unclipped the mic from her shirt as she stood. She placed the mic carefully on the chair. "No comment," she said, and left the room before the interviewer could see the tears in her eyes.

In Shanghai, Olive spent a combined total of three hours talking about herself and about her book, which meant talking about the end of the world while trying not to imagine the world ending with her daughter in it, and then returned to her hotel, where she noticed in the corridor that she was having difficulty walking in a straight line. She never drank, but drunkenness and fatigue look the same sometimes. Olive weaved down the hallway and stumbled into her room. She closed the door behind her and stood just inside for a long time, her forehead resting on the cool wall above the light switch. After a while, she heard her own voice, repeating *It's too much. It's too much. It's too much.*

"Olive," the room's AI system said softly, when some time had passed, "do you desire assistance?" When Olive didn't answer, it repeated the inquiry in Mandarin and Cantonese.

"Olive, this is totally random, but I was your agent's babysitter," a woman told her, in a signing line in Singapore the next day.

· · ·

"What message would you like your readers to take away from *Marienbad*?" another interviewer asked.

Olive and the interviewer were onstage together in Tokyo. The interviewer was a hologram, because for unspecified personal reasons he'd been unable to leave Nairobi. Olive suspected the personal reason was illness: the interviewer kept freezing up, but the sound had no lag, which meant the interviewer wasn't freezing due to a bad connection, he was freezing because he kept pressing the Cough button on his console.

"I was just trying to write an interesting book," Olive said. "There's no message."

"Are you sure?" the interviewer asked.

"Will you sign a used book?" a woman asked, in a signing line.

"Of course, I'd be happy to."

"Also," the woman said, "is this your handwriting?"

Someone, not Olive, had already written in this woman's copy of *Marienbad*: *Harold: I enjoyed last night. xoxoxoxo Olive Llewellyn.*

Olive stared at the message and felt just a touch of vertigo. "No," she said, "I don't know who wrote that."

(She was distracted for days afterward by the thought of a shadow Olive moving over the landscape, on a kind of parallel tour, writing uncharacteristic messages in Olive's books.)

. . .

In Cape Town, Olive met an author who'd been out on the road with his husband for a year and a half, touring in the service of a book that had sold several times as many copies as *Marienbad*.

"We're trying to see how long we can travel until we have to go home," the author said. His name was Ibby, short for Ibrahim, and his husband was Jack. The three of them were sitting together in the evening on the rooftop terrace of the hotel, which was filled with authors attending a literary festival.

"Are you trying to avoid going home?" Olive asked. "Or you just like travelling?"

"Both," Jack said. "I like being on the road."

"And our apartment's mediocre," Ibby said, "but we haven't decided what to do about it. Move? Redecorate? Could go either way."

There were dozens of trees up here, in enormous planters, with little lights sparkling in the branches. Music was playing somewhere, a string quartet. Olive was wearing her designated fancy tour dress, which was silver and went to her ankles. *This is one of the glamorous moments,* Olive thought, filing it carefully away so she could draw on it for sustenance later. The breeze carried a scent of jasmine.

"*I* heard some good news today," Jack said.

"Tell me," Ibby said. "I've been in a kind of book festival tunnel all day. Inadvertent news blackout."

"Construction just began on the first of the Far Colonies," Jack said.

Olive smiled, and almost spoke, but she was momentarily wordless. Planning for the Far Colonies had begun when her grandparents were children. She would always remember this moment, she thought, this party, these people whom she very much liked and might never see again. She'd be able to tell Sylvie where she was when she heard the news. When had she last experienced true awe? It had been a while. Olive was flooded with happiness. She raised her glass.

"To Alpha Centauri," she said.

In Buenos Aires, Olive met a woman who wanted to show her a tattoo. "I hope this isn't weird," she said, and rolled up her sleeve to reveal a quote from the book: *We knew it was coming*, in a beautiful curly script on her left shoulder.

Olive's breath caught in her throat. It wasn't just a line from *Marienbad*, it was a tattoo in *Marienbad*. In the second half of the novel, her character Gaspery-Jacques had the line tattooed on his left arm. You write a book with a fictional tattoo and then the tattoo becomes real in the world and after that almost anything seems possible. She'd seen five of those tattoos, but that didn't make it less extraordinary, seeing the way fiction can bleed into the world and leave a mark on someone's skin.

"That's incredible," Olive said softly. "It's incredible to see that tattoo in the real world."

"It's my favourite line from your book," she said. "It's just true of so much, isn't it?"

. . .

But doesn't everything seem obvious in retrospect? Blue dusk over the prairies, gliding toward the Dakota Republic in a low-altitude airship. Olive stared out the window and tried to find some peace in the landscape. She had a new invitation for a festival on Titan. She hadn't been since she was a kid and retained only vague memories of crowds at the Dolphinarium and some oddly tasteless popcorn, the warm yellowish haze of the daytime sky—she'd been in a so-called Realist colony, one of the outposts whose settlers had decided on clear domes in order to experience the true colours of the Titanian atmosphere—and strange fashions, this thing all the teenagers were doing that involved painting their faces like pixels, big squares of colour that were supposed to defeat the facial-recognition software but that had the side effect of making them look like deranged clowns. Should she go to Titan? *I want to go home.* Where was Sylvie at this moment? *This is easier than having a day job, though, just remember that.*

"I remember reading somewhere," an interviewer said, "that the title of your first book actually came from your last day job?"

"Yes," Olive said, "I came across it at work one day."

"Your first novel was, of course, *Swimming Stars with Gold-flitter.* Will you tell me about that title?"

"Sure, yes. I was working in AI training. So, you know, correcting awkward renderings from the translator bots. I remember sitting there by the hour in this cramped little office—"

"This was in Colony Two?"

"Yes, Colony Two. My job was to sit there all day, rewording unfortunate sentences. But there was one that stopped me cold, because it may have been awkward and error-ridden, but I loved it." Olive had told this story so often that it was like reciting lines from a play. "It was a description of votive candles with little poems on the candleholders. The description had somehow been rendered as *seven motives for verse,* and then one of the candle descriptions was *swimming stars with goldflitter.* The beauty of those phrases, I don't know, it just stopped me cold."

Stopped me cold. Two days later she was on a panel with another writer at a festival in the city-state of Los Angeles, and the implication of that phrase had just occurred to her. What stops you, and turns you cold? Death, obviously. Olive couldn't believe she'd never thought of this. Los Angeles was under a dome, but still the light through the windows was blinding. This meant she couldn't see the audience, which was frankly ideal. All those faces staring at her. No, at them: the other writer's name was Jessica Marley and Olive was glad Jessica was here with her, even though she didn't actually like her very much. Everything offended Jessica, which is inevitable when you move through the world in search of offence.

"Well, some of us don't have doctorates in literature, Jim," Jessica said to the interviewer, in response to some imperceptible provocation. The look on his face mirrored Olive's thought at that moment: *Well, that escalated quickly.* But a man in the audience was standing up with a question about *Marienbad.* Almost all of the questions were about *Marienbad,* which was awkward because Jessica was there too, Jessica with her book about coming of age in the moon colonies. Olive was pretending that she hadn't read *Moon/Rise,* because she'd hated it. Olive had lived the real thing, and it wasn't nearly as poetic as Jessica's book suggested. Growing up in a moon colony was fine. It was neither great nor dystopian. It was a little house in a pleasant neighbourhood of tree-lined streets, a good but not extraordinary public school, life lived at a consistent 15° to 22° Celsius under carefully calibrated dome lighting, scheduled rainfalls. She didn't grow up *longing for Earth* or experience her life as *a continual displacement,* thank you.

"I wanted to ask Olive about the death of the prophet in *Marienbad,*" the man in the audience said. Jessica sighed and slumped a little in her chair. "It could have been a much bigger moment, but you decided to make it a relatively small, not-climactic event."

"Really? I thought of it as climactic," Olive said, as mildly as possible.

He smiled, humouring her. "But you chose to make it really small, almost inconsequential, when it could have been cinematic, something really big. Why is that?"

Jessica sat up straight, excited by the possibility of combat.

"Well," Olive said. "I suppose everyone has a different idea of what constitutes a big moment."

"You're a master of deflection," Jessica murmured, without looking at her. "You're like some kind of deflection ninja."

"Thank you," Olive said, although she knew it wasn't a compliment.

"Let's move on to the next question," the interviewer said.

"You know the phrase I keep thinking about?" a poet asked, on a different panel, at a festival in Copenhagen. " 'The chickens are coming home to roost.' Because it's never good chickens. It's never 'You've been a good person and now your chickens are coming home to roost.' It's never good chickens. It's always bad chickens."

Scattered laughter and applause. A man in the audience was having a coughing fit. He left quickly, bent over in an apologetic way. Olive wrote *no good chickens* in the margin of her festival program.

Was the death of the prophet in *Marienbad* too anticlimactic? It seemed possible. Olive was sitting alone at a hotel bar near the Copenhagen festival, drinking tea and eating a wilted salad with too much cheese on it. On the one hand the prophet's death *was* dramatic, after all he'd been shot in the head, but maybe there should've been some kind of battle scene, maybe the death really was too casual, in the way he went from perfect health to death over the course of a paragraph and the story kept moving without him—

"May I get you anything else?" the bartender asked.

"Just the check, please," Olive said.

—but on the other hand, isn't that reality? Won't most of

us die in fairly unclimactic ways, our passing unremarked by almost everyone, our deaths becoming plot points in the narratives of the people around us? But obviously *Marienbad* was fiction, i.e., reality wasn't relevant to the question at hand, and maybe the death of the prophet really was a flaw. Now Olive was holding the pen over the check, but there was a difficulty: she'd forgotten her room number. She had to go to the front desk to retrieve it.

"It happens more often than you'd think," the clerk at the front desk said.

At the airship terminal the next morning, she sat next to a business traveller who wanted to tell her about his job, which had something to do with detecting counterfeit steel. Olive listened for a long time, because the monologue distracted her from how much she missed Sylvie. "And what do you do?" the other traveller asked finally.

"I write books," Olive said.

"For children?" he asked.

When Olive circled back to the Atlantic Republic, seeing her AR publicist again was like seeing an old friend. Aretta and Olive sat together at a dinner for booksellers in Jersey City.

"How's it been since I saw you last?" Aretta asked.

"Fine," Olive said, "it's all going fine. I have no complaints." And then, because she was tired and she knew Aretta a little by now, she broke her own rule about never revealing anything personal, and said, "It's just a lot of people."

Aretta smiled. "Publicists aren't supposed to be shy," she said, "but I get a little overwhelmed at these dinners sometimes."

"Me too," Olive said. "My face gets tired."

That night's hotel room was white and blue. The thing with being away from her husband and daughter was that every hotel room was emptier than the one before.

The last interview of the tour was the following afternoon in Philadelphia, where Olive met a man in a dark suit who was her age or a little younger, in a beautiful meeting room at a hotel. The room was on a high floor with a wall of glass, and the city rolled away beneath them.

"Here we are," said Aretta brightly. "Olive, this is Gaspery Roberts, *Contingencies Magazine*. I have to make a couple of quick calls, so I'll leave you two." She receded. Olive and the interviewer sat in matching green velvet chairs.

"Thank you for meeting with me," the man said.

"My pleasure. Do you mind if I ask about your name? I'm not sure I've ever met a Gaspery."

"I'll tell you something even stranger," he said. "My first name is actually Gaspery-Jacques."

"Seriously? I thought I'd made up the name for that character in *Marienbad*."

He smiled. "My mother was astonished when she came across the name in your book. She thought she'd made it up too."

"Perhaps I came across your name somewhere and didn't consciously remember it."

"Anything's possible. It's hard to know what we know sometimes, isn't it?" He had a gentle way of speaking that Olive liked, and a faint accent that she couldn't quite place. "Have you been in interviews all day?"

"Half the day. You're my fifth."

"Ouch. I'll keep this brief, then. I'd like to ask you about a specific scene in *Marienbad,* if I may."

"Okay. Sure."

"The scene in the spaceport," he said. "Where your character Willis hears the violin and he's . . . transported."

"It's an odd passage," Olive said. "I get a lot of questions about it."

"I'd like to ask you something." Gaspery hesitated. "This might seem a bit—I don't mean to pry. But is there an element of—I'm wondering if that bit of the book was inspired by a personal experience."

"I've never been interested in auto-fiction," Olive said, but it was difficult to meet his eyes now. She'd always found something steadying in looking at her own clasped hands, but she didn't know if it was the hands or the shirt, the impeccable white cuffs. Clothes are armour.

"Listen," Gaspery said, "I don't mean to make you uncomfortable or put you on the spot. But I'm curious if you experienced something strange in the Oklahoma City Airship Terminal."

In the quiet, Olive could hear the soft hum of the building, the sounds of ventilation and plumbing. Perhaps she wouldn't have admitted it if he hadn't caught her toward the end of the tour, if she hadn't been so tired.

"I don't mind talking about this," she said, "but I'm afraid I'll seem too eccentric if it makes it into the final version of the interview. Could we go off the record for a moment?"

"Yes," he said.

Bad Chickens /

2401

1

No star burns forever. You can say "It's the end of the world" and mean it, but what gets lost in that kind of careless usage is that the world will eventually literally end. Not "civilization," whatever that is, but the actual planet.

Which is not to say that those smaller endings aren't annihilating. A year before I began my training at the Time Institute, I went to a dinner party at my friend Ephrem's place. He was just back from a vacation on Earth, and he had a story about going on a walk in a cemetery with his daughter, Meiying, who was four at the time. Ephrem was an arborist. He liked to go to old cemeteries to look at the trees. But then they found the grave of another four-year-old girl, Ephrem told me, and he just wanted to leave after that. He was used to graveyards, he sought them out, he'd always said he didn't find them depressing, just peaceful, but that one grave just got to him. He looked at it and was unbearably sad. Also it was the worst kind of Earth summer day, impossibly humid, and he felt like he couldn't get enough air. The drone of the cicadas was oppressive. Sweat ran down his back. He told his daughter it was time to go, but she lingered by the gravestone for a moment.

"If her parents loved her," Meiying said, "it would have felt like the end of the world."

It was such an eerily astute observation, Ephrem told me, that he stood there staring at her and found himself thinking, *Where did you come from?* They got out of the cemetery with difficulty—"She had to stop and inspect every goddamned flower and pinecone," he said—and never went back.

Those are the worlds that end in our day-to-day lives, these stopped children, these annihilating losses, but at the end of Earth there will be actual, literal annihilation, hence the colonies. The first colony on the moon was intended as a prototype, a practice run for establishing a presence in other solar systems in the coming centuries. "Because we'll have to," the president of China said, at the press conference where construction on the first colony was announced, "eventually, whether we want to or not, unless we want all of human history and achievement to get sucked into a supernova a few million years down the line."

I watched footage of that press conference in my sister Zoey's office, three hundred years after the fact. The president behind the lectern with her officials arrayed around her, a crowd of reporters below the stage. One of them raised his hand: "Are we sure it's going to be a supernova?"

"Of course not," the president said. "It could be anything. Rogue planet, asteroid storm, you name it. The point is that we're orbiting a star, and all stars eventually die."

"But if the star dies," I said to Zoey, "obviously the Earth's moon goes with it."

"Sure," she said, "but we're just the prototype, Gaspery. We're just proof of concept. The Far Colonies have been populated for a hundred and eighty years."

2

The first moon colony was built on the silent flatlands of the Sea of Tranquility, near where the Apollo 11 astronauts had landed in a long-ago century. Their flag was still there, in the distance, a fragile little statue on the windless surface.

There was substantial interest in immigration to the colony. Earth was so crowded by then, and such swaths of it had been rendered uninhabitable by flooding or heat. The colony's architects had set aside space for substantial residential development, which sold out quickly. The developers lobbied successfully for a second colony when they ran out of space in Colony One. But Colony Two was built a little too hastily, and within a century the lighting system on the main dome had failed. The lighting system was meant to mimic the appearance of the sky as viewed from Earth—it was nice to look up and see blue, as opposed to looking up into the void—and when it failed there was no more false atmosphere, no more shifting pixelations to give the impression of clouds, no more carefully calibrated preprogrammed sunrises and sunsets, no more blue. Which is not to suggest that there wasn't light, but that light was extremely un-Earthlike: on a bright day, the colonists looked up into space. The juxtaposition of utter darkness with bright light made some people dizzy, although whether this was physical or psychological was up for debate. More seriously, the failure of the dome lighting removed the illusion of the twenty-four-hour day. Now the sun rose rapidly and spent two weeks crossing the sky, after which there were two straight weeks of night.

The cost of repair was deemed prohibitive. There was a degree of adaptation—bedroom windows were outfitted with shutters, so people could sleep during the nights when the sun was out, and street lighting was improved for the days without sunlight— but property values declined, and most people who could afford it moved to Colony One or the recently completed Colony Three. "Colony Two" drifted out of common parlance; everyone called it the Night City. It was the place where the sky was always black.

I grew up in the Night City. My walk to school took me past the childhood home of Olive Llewellyn, an author who'd walked those same streets two hundred years ago, not too far out from the moon's first settlers. It was a little house on a tree-lined street, and I could tell that it had been pretty once, but the neighbourhood had gone downhill since Olive Llewellyn had been a child there. The house was a wreck now, half the windows covered up and graffiti everywhere, but the plaque by the front door remained. I paid the house no attention, until my mother told me she'd named me after a peripheral character in *Marienbad,* Llewellyn's most famous book. I didn't read the book— I didn't like books—but my sister Zoey did and reported back: the Gaspery-Jacques in the book wasn't anything like me.

I decided not to ask her what she meant. I was eleven when she read it, which would have made her thirteen or fourteen. By then she was already a serious, driven kind of person who was obviously going to excel at everything she attempted, whereas by eleven I already had the first suspicions that I might not be exactly the kind of person I wanted to be, and it would be awful if she were to tell me that the other Gaspery-Jacques were, say, a strikingly handsome and generally impressive person who was extremely focused on his schoolwork and never committed petty theft. But nonetheless I began to secretly regard Olive Llewellyn's childhood home with a degree of respect. I felt connected to it.

There was a family living there, a boy and a girl and their parents, pale, miserable-looking people who possessed this weird talent for conveying an impression that they were up to no good. They had an air of having gone to seed, the whole family. Their last name was Anderson. The parents spent a lot of time on the porch, arguing quietly or staring into space. The boy was surly and got into fights at school. The girl, who was about my age, liked to play with a hologram in the front yard, an old-fashioned mirror hologram who danced with her sometimes, and that was actually the only time I saw the Anderson girl smile anywhere near her house, when she was spinning and leaping and her holographic double was spinning and leaping too.

When I was twelve, the Anderson girl was in the same class as me, and I learned her name was Talia. Who was Talia Anderson? She loved to draw. She did backflips on the field. She looked much happier at school than she did at home.

"I know you," she said abruptly one day, when we were in the cafeteria line together. "You're always walking by my house."

"It's on my way," I said.

"On your way to what?"

"Well, on my way to everywhere. I live at the end of the cul-de-sac."

"I know," she said.

"How do you know where I live?"

"I walk by your house too," she said. "I cut through your neighbour's lawn to get to the Periphery."

At the end of our lawn there was a screen of leaves. Push through them and you'd get to the Periphery Road, which circled the interior of the Night City dome. Cross the road and there was a strange, wild area, no more than fifty feet deep, a strip of wilderness between the road and the dome. Scrub brush, dust, stray plants, garbage. It was a forgotten kind of place. Our mother didn't like us playing there, so Zoey never ventured across the Periphery Road—she always did as she was told, which I found maddening—but I liked the wildness of it, the mild sense of danger inherent in a forgotten kingdom. That day after school

I crossed the empty road for the first time in a few weeks, and stood for a while with my hands pressed to the dome, looking out. The composite glass was so thick that everything on the other side looked like a dream, distant in a muffled kind of way, but I saw craters here and there, meteors, grey. The opaque dome of Colony One glowed in the near distance. I found myself wondering what Talia Anderson's thoughts were when she gazed out at the moonscape.

Talia Anderson transferred out of my class and left the neighbourhood halfway through the year. I didn't see her again until my mid-thirties, when we were both employed by the Grand Luna Hotel in Colony One.

I started work at the hotel about a month after my mother died. She'd been sick for a long time, years, and at the end Zoey and I all but lived at the hospital. That last week we were there every day and every night, exhausted comrades keeping watch, while our mother murmured and slept. Death was imminent and remained imminent, for much longer than the doctors predicted. Our mother had worked at the post office since we were very young, but in her last hours she thought she was doing postdoctoral work in a physics lab again, murmuring in a confused way about equations and the simulation hypothesis.

"Do you understand what she's talking about?" I asked Zoey at one point.

"Most of it," Zoey said. In those hours Zoey sat by the bed

with her eyes closed, listening to our mother's words as if listening to music.

"Can you explain it to me?" It was like being on the outside of a secret club, nose pressed to the glass.

"The simulation hypothesis? Yeah." She didn't open her eyes. "Think of how holograms and virtual reality have evolved, even just in the past few years. If we can run fairly convincing simulations of reality now, think of what those simulations will be like in a century or two. The idea with the simulation hypothesis is, we can't rule out the possibility that all of reality is a simulation."

I'd been awake for two days and felt like I was dreaming. "Okay, but if we're living in a computer," I said, "whose computer is it?"

"Who knows? Humans, a few hundred years into the future? An alien intelligence? It's not a mainstream theory, but it comes up every so often at the Time Institute." She opened her eyes. "Oh god, pretend I didn't say that. I'm tired. I shouldn't have."

"Pretend you didn't say what?"

"The Time Institute part."

"Okay," I said, and her eyes closed again. I closed my eyes too. Our mother had stopped murmuring, and now there were just her ragged breaths, with too much time between each one.

When at last the end came, Zoey and I were sleeping. She woke me in the exhausted grey light of early morning, and we sat together for a long time in silence, in reverence, before the stilled figure of our mother on the bed. We dealt with the formalities, hugged goodbye, went our separate ways. I returned home to my cramped apartment, and several days passed where I spoke only with my cat. There was the funeral, then more stillness. I needed a new job—I'd been without one for some time and was burning through my savings—and so a month after the funeral I found myself in the basement office of a hotel Human Resources officer, a vaguely familiar-looking woman with blond hair, accepting a position that had been advertised as "hotel detective" but whose exact parameters were unclear.

"To be absolutely honest," I told her, "I'm not entirely clear on what a hotel detective position might entail."

"It's just hotel security," she said. I realized I'd forgotten her name. Natalie? Natasha? "The job title wasn't my idea. You won't actually be a detective. Just a security presence, as it were."

"I want to be sure I'm not misrepresenting myself," I said. "I left school a few months shy of my criminal justice degree."

"Can we be honest here, Gaspery?" There was definitely something familiar about her.

"Please."

"Your entire job is to pay attention to what goes on around you and call the police if you see anything suspicious."

"I can do that."

"You sound doubtful," she said.

"I'm not doubtful for myself. I mean, I don't doubt I could do it. It's just, I'm—couldn't anyone do this job?"

"You'd be surprised. It's the attention part that's hard to hire for," she said. "Distraction is a problem, generally speaking. You remember that test you had to take on your first interview?"

"Sure."

"That was to measure attentiveness. Your score was high. Tell me, do you agree with your test results? Can you pay attention?"

"Yes," I said. I was pleased as I said this, because I'd never really thought of myself in this way before, but it seemed to me that I'd been paying close attention my entire life. I hadn't been successful at very many things, but I'd always been good at watching. That was how I knew my ex-wife had fallen in love with someone else, just by being attentive. There were no obvious clues, just a subtle shift in— but the HR person was talking again, so I reeled myself in from the past.

"Wait," I said. "I know you."

"From before this meeting, you mean?"

"Talia," I said.

Something changed in her face. A mask dropped. Her voice was different when she spoke again, less amused by the world. "I go by Natalia now, but yes." She was quiet for a moment, looking at me. "We went to school together, didn't we?"

"End of the cul-de-sac," I said, and for the first time in the interview, she gave me a genuine smile.

"I used to stand at the Periphery for hours," she said, "looking out through the glass."

"You ever go back there? To the Night City?"

"Never," she said.

3

Never to the Night City. The phrase had a rhythm that pleased me, so it lodged itself in my head. I thought of it often in my first weeks on the job, because the job was terminally boring. The hotel had retro pretensions, so I wore a suit cut in an antique style and a peculiarly shaped hat called a fedora. I walked the halls and stood watch in the lobby. I paid attention to everyone and everything, as instructed. I've always enjoyed watching other people, but people in hotels turned out to be surprisingly boring. They checked in and checked out. They appeared in the lobby at odd hours, asking for coffee. They were drunk, or they weren't. They were businesspeople, or they were with their families on vacation. They were tired and frazzled from their journeys. People tried to sneak in dogs. In the first six months I had to summon the police only once, when I heard a woman scream in a hotel room, and even then I wasn't the one who did the calling;

I called the night manager, who called the police for me. I wasn't there when the woman was carried out by paramedics.

The job was quiet. My mind wandered. *Never to the Night City*. What had Talia's life been like there? Not great, obviously, any idiot could see that. Some families are better than others. When her family moved out of the Olive Llewellyn house, some other family moved in, but I found I couldn't remember this other family beyond a general impression of dereliction. At the hotel I saw Talia only occasionally, passing through the lobby on her way home from work.

In those days I lived in a bland little apartment in a block of other bland little apartments on the far edge of Colony One, close enough to the Periphery that the dome barely cleared the roof of the apartment complex. Sometimes on dark nights I liked to cross the street to the Periphery, to look through the composite glass at Colony Two glittering in the distance. My life in those days was as bland and limited as my apartment. I tried not to think about my mother too much. I slept through the days. My cat always woke me in the late afternoon. Around sunset I ate a meal that could reasonably be called either dinner or breakfast, put on my uniform, and went to the hotel to stare at people for seven hours.

I'd been at the hotel for about six months when my sister turned thirty-seven. Zoey was a physicist at the university, and her area of expertise had something to do with quantum blockchain technology, which I was never able to understand although she'd made several good-faith efforts to explain it to me. I called to wish her a happy birthday, and realized in the beat before she picked up that I hadn't congratulated her on receiving tenure. Which was when, a month ago? I felt a familiar variety of guilt.

"Happy Birthday," I said. "And also congratulations."

"Thank you, Gaspery." She never dwelt on my lapses, and I couldn't entirely parse why this made me feel so awful. There's a low-level, specific pain in having to accept that putting up with you requires a certain generosity of spirit in your loved ones.

"What's it like?"

"Being thirty-seven?" She sounded tired.

"No, being tenured. Does it feel different?"

"It feels like stability," she said.

"So what are your birthday plans?"

She was quiet for a moment. "Gaspery," she said, "is there any way you could come to my office this evening?"

"Of course," I said. "Of course."

When had she ever asked me to her office? Just once, years ago, when she first started there. The university wasn't that far away from my apartment, but also it was fundamentally a different universe. When had I even seen her last? It had been a few months, I realized.

I called in sick to work and then lay on the sofa for a while to bask in my sudden freedom. Marvin, my cat, climbed heavily onto my chest, where he stretched out his legs and fell asleep purring. The night extended before me, all those magnificently empty hours shining with possibility. I dislodged Marvin, showered and put on nice clothes, stopped by a bakery for four cupcakes—red velvet, which I hoped was still Zoey's favourite— and by six-thirty p.m. the sun was setting in a wash of oranges and pinks on the far side of the dome. I'd lived for a year in Colony One and the dome lighting still looked like theatre to me. Were cupcakes enough? Should I buy flowers? I bought a bouquet of something unflashy and yellow, and was at the Time Institute gate by seven thirty. I took off my dark glasses for the iris scan and was still holding the glasses awkwardly in my hand six iris scans later, when I found Zoey pacing in her office. She didn't look like a woman celebrating a birthday. She took my flowers with a distracted air, and I could tell from the way she set them on her desk that she'd forgotten about them by the time they left her hand. I wondered if someone had just broken up with her, but Zoey's romantic life had always been a forbidden topic.

"Oh, thank god," she said when I held out a cupcake. "I completely forgot dinner."

"You seem agitated."

"Can I show you something?"

"Sure."

She touched a discreet console on her office wall, and a projection filled half the room. There was a man on a stage, surrounded by bulky antique machines of some kind, inscrutable instruments. Above his head was an old-fashioned screen, a rectangle of white floating there in the dim light. It seemed to me that the scene we were looking at was quite old.

"A friend sent this to me," Zoey said. "She works in the art history department."

"Who is he? The guy in the projection."

"Paul James Smith. Twenty-first-century composer and video artist."

She pressed play, and the room filled with three-hundred-year-old music in a vague, shifting genre. Ambient, I supposed. I didn't know much about music but found this guy's composition faintly annoying.

"Okay," she said, "now pay attention to the white screen above him."

"What am I looking for? It's blank."

"Watch."

The screen came to life. The video had been shot in a forest on Earth. The quality was a little jerky; the videographer had been walking on a forest path, toward an enormous leafy tree, some Earth species that didn't grow in the colonies. The music stopped, and the man looked up at the screen above him. The screen went dark. There was a strange cacophony of noise—notes of a violin, the indistinct murmur of a crowd, the hydraulic *whoosh* of an airship taking off—and then it was over, the forest was back, and for a moment the image was dizzying, as if the videographer had forgotten that they were holding a camera. The forest faded out, but the music continued.

"Listen carefully," Zoey said. "Listen to the way the music's changed. You hear how the violin notes from the video are there in Smith's music? That same motif, that five-note pattern?"

I couldn't hear it, and then I could. "Yes. Why is that important?"

"Because it means that . . . that weirdness, that glitch, whatever it was, it was part of the performance. It's not a technical problem." She stopped the recording. She looked troubled in a way I didn't understand. "It goes on," she said, "but the rest of the performance is uninteresting."

"You brought me here to show me that," I said, just checking.

"I need to talk this through with someone I trust." She picked up her device, and I heard my own device chime with an incoming document.

She'd sent me a book: *Marienbad,* by Olive Llewellyn.

"Mom's favourite novel," I said. I was thinking of our mother, reading on the porch at twilight.

"Have you read it, Gaspery?"

"I've never been much of a reader."

"Just jump to the highlighted passage and tell me if you notice anything."

It was disorienting, leaping into the middle of a book I'd never read. I started a few paragraphs before the passage she'd highlighted:

We knew it was coming.

We knew it was coming and we prepared accordingly, or at least that's what we told our children—and ourselves—in the decades that followed.

We knew it was coming but we didn't quite believe it, so we prepared in low-key, unobtrusive ways—"Why do we have a whole shelf of canned fish?" Willis asked his husband, who said something vague about emergency preparedness—

—Because of that ancient horror, too embarrassingly irrational to be articulated aloud: if you say the name of the thing you fear, might you attract that thing's attention? This is difficult to admit, but in those early weeks we were vague about our fears because saying the word *pandemic* might bend the pandemic toward us.

We knew it was coming and we were breezy about it. We deflected the fear with careless bravado. On the day reports broke of a cluster in Vancouver, which was three days after the British prime minister announced that the initial outbreak in London was fully contained, Willis and Dov went to work as usual, their sons Isaac and Sam went to school, and then they all met up for dinner at their favourite restaurant, which was crowded that night. (Bit of a horror movie in retrospect: imagine clouds of invisible pathogens drifting through the air, floating from table to table, swirling in the wake of passing servers.) "If it's in Vancouver it's obviously here," Dov said to Willis, who said, "I'd bet money on it," and refilled Dov's water glass.

"If what's in Vancouver?" Isaac asked. He was nine.

"Nothing," they said in unison, and felt no guilt at all because it didn't feel like a lie. Pandemics don't approach like wars, with the distant thud of artillery growing louder every day and flashes of bombs on the horizon. They arrive in *retrospect*, essentially. It's disorienting. The pandemic is far away and then it's all around you, with seemingly no intermediate step.

Dov, practising his lines in front of the bedroom mirror after the community theatre closed: "Is this the promised end?"

We knew it was coming but we behaved inconsistently. We stocked up on supplies—just in case—but sent our children to school, because how do you get any work done with the kids at home?

(We were still thinking in terms of getting work done. The most shocking thing in retrospect was the degree to which all of us completely missed the point.)

"God," Willis said, a few days before the schools closed, but after the news headlines had started, "this all seems so retro."

"I know," Dov said. They were both in their forties, which is to say they were old enough to remember Ebola X, but those sixty-four weeks of lockdown had faded to the hazy province of childhood memory, a span of time that was neither awful nor pleasant, months populated by cartoons and imaginary friends. You couldn't call it a lost year, because it did have nice moments. Their parents were competent enough at parenting to shield them from the horror, which meant it was lonely but not unbearable. There was a lot of ice cream and extra screen time. They'd been glad when it was over, but after a few years had passed they didn't think of it much.

"What does *retro* mean?" Sam asked.

As Willis glanced at his younger son, he did have the thought—he clung to this later—that perhaps school wasn't such a great idea. Nonetheless, the old world hadn't slipped away just yet, so in the morning he packed Sam's and Isaac's lunches and dropped them off at the academy, stepped back out into the bright sunlight, and caught a transporter to the airship terminal. Just an ordinary morning under a harmless blue sky.

In the terminal he stopped to listen to a musician, a violinist playing for spare change in one of the cavernous entry corridors. The violinist was an old man who played with his eyes closed, coins accumulating in a hat by his feet. He played an ancient-looking violin—it looked like it was made of real wood—and Willis was by no means an expert in acoustics, but it seemed to him that there was a kind of warmth in the sound. Willis was listening to the music, to the way it rose up over the susurration of the morning commuter crowd, but then—

—a flash of darkness, weird sudden light—

—a fleeting hallucination of forest, fresh air, trees rising around him, a summer's day—

—and then he was back in the Oklahoma City Airship Terminal, in the cool white of the west entry corridor, blinking
and disoriented. *Something just came over me,* he found himself
thinking, but this was inadequate as an explanation, because
what had just come over him? That flash of darkness, then the
forest rising around him, what was that?

It hit him all at once: an afterlife.

The darkness was death, he told himself. The forest was the
after.

Willis didn't believe in an actual afterlife, but he did believe in
the subconscious, he believed in knowing without consciously
knowing, and almost without thought he was walking away in
the wrong direction, away from his commute. He didn't know
where he was going until he found himself on the doorstep of
his sons' school.

"But why are you pulling your boys out of school?" the prin-
cipal asked. "I've been following the news closely, Willis, and
there's just that tiny cluster of cases in Vancouver."

I closed the file and put my device in my pocket, unsettled in a
way I couldn't explain.

"Do you see it?" Zoey asked. "The way the video mirrors the
passage in the book?"

I did see it. A person in a forest in the twenty-first century sees a flash of darkness and hears noises from an airship terminal two centuries later. A person in an airship terminal in the twenty-third century sees a flash of darkness and is struck by the overwhelming sensation that he's standing in a forest.

"She could have seen the video," I suggested. "Olive Llewellyn, I mean. She could've seen it and worked it into her fiction." I was pleased with myself for this suggestion.

"I thought of that," Zoey said. *Of course you did,* I didn't say aloud. That was a major difference between us: Zoey always thought of everything. "There's something else, though. My team's spent the last month researching the region where the composer grew up, and this afternoon we found a letter." She was scrolling through files on her projection, but it was set to privacy mode, so it appeared from my angle that she was moving her hand through clouds. "Here," she said.

A projection snapped into place in the air between us. It was a handwritten document in a foreign alphabet.

"What is this?"

"I think it might be supporting evidence. It's a letter," she said. "From 1912."

"What alphabet's this?" I asked.

"Seriously?"

"What, should I be able to read it?" I peered closer, and recognized a word. No, two. It was almost English, but warped and slanted; there was a certain beauty to it, but the letters were misformed. Some kind of proto-English?

"Gaspery, that's cursive," she said.

"I don't know what that is."

"Right," she said, with that maddening patience I'd come to expect from her. "Let me switch to audio."

She toggled something in the clouds, and a man's voice filled the room.

Bert,

Thank you for your kind letter of 25th April, which made its way across the Atlantic and across Canada at a snail's pace and arrived in my hands only this evening.

How am I, you ask? The honest answer, brother, is that I'm unsure. This comes to you from a candlelit room in Victoria— you'll forgive, I hope, the dash of melodrama, but I feel that I've earned it—where I've taken up lodging in a pleasant boarding-house. I have given up all thought of establishing myself in business and wish only to return home, but this is a comfortable exile and my remittance provides for my day-to-day necessities.

I've had a very strange time here. No, that's not quite it. I've had a somewhat dull time here—my fault, not Canada's—except for a strange interlude in the wilderness, which I shall attempt to recount. I had travelled north from Victoria with Niall's old friend from school, Thomas Maillot, whose surname I'm possibly mis-spelling. For two or three days we moved north up the coast on a tidy little steamboat, weighed down with provisions, until at last we arrived at Caiette, a village consisting of a church, a pier, a one-room schoolhouse, and a handful of houses. Thomas continued on to a logging camp, a short distance up the coast. I elected to remain for the moment in the boardinghouse in Caiette, for the sake of enjoying the beauty of that place.

One morning in early September, I ventured into the forest, for reasons too tedious to relate, and a few paces in, I came upon a maple tree. I stopped there a moment, to catch my breath, and then there occurred an incident that struck me at the time as some kind of supernatural event, but seems to me in retrospect to have been perhaps some kind of fit.

I was standing there in the forest in the sunlight, and then all at once there was darkness, as abruptly as a candle snuffed out in a room, and in the darkness I heard the notes of a violin, an inscrutable noise, and with this a strange impression of being somehow fleetingly indoors, in some echoing cavernous space like a train station. Then it was over and I stood in the forest. It was as though nothing had happened. I staggered back out to the beach and was violently sick on the rocks. The following morning, concerned for my well-being and determined to quit that place and return to some semblance of civilization, I began the return journey to the little city of Victoria, where I remain.

I have a perfectly adequate room at a boardinghouse by the harbour, and amuse myself with walks, books, chess, and the occasional bit of watercolour painting. As you know, I've always adored gardens, and there's a public garden here in which I've found great solace. Not to trouble anyone, but I did consult a doctor, who is confident in his diagnosis of migraine. Seems a peculiar sort of

migraine that doesn't involve any pain in one's head, but I suppose
I'll accept it in lieu of an alternate explanation. I cannot forget it,
however, and the memory unsettles me.

I hope you are well, Bert. Please convey my affection and respect
to Mother and Father as well.

Yours,

Edwin

The audio stopped. Zoey swiped the projection into the wall and came to sit with me. There was a heaviness about her that I'd never seen before.

"Zoey," I said, "you seem more upset than . . . I'm not sure I completely understand."

"Which operating system do you use on your device?"

"Zephyr," I said.

"Same. You remember that weird Zephyr bug a couple years ago, this only lasted a day or two, but sometimes you'd open a text file on your device and you'd hear whatever music you'd been listening to last?"

"Sure. That was annoying." I only vaguely remembered it.

"It was file corruption."

I sensed something vast and terrible, swimming just outside of my grasp.

"You're saying . . ."

Zoey's elbows were on the table, and as she spoke, she rested her forehead in her hands.

"If moments from different centuries are bleeding into one another, then, well, one way you could think of those moments, Gaspery, is to think of them as corrupted files."

"How is a moment the same as a file?"

She was very still. "Just imagine that they are."

I tried. A series of corrupted files; a series of corrupted moments; a series of discrete things bleeding into one another when they shouldn't.

"But if moments are files . . ." I couldn't finish the sentence. The room we were in seemed much less real than it had only a moment ago. *The desk is real,* I told myself. *The wilted flowers on the desk are real. The blue paint on the walls. Zoey's hair. My hands. The carpet.*

"You see why I didn't go out to celebrate my birthday," she said.

"It's just . . . Look, I agree that it's weird, but we're talking about Mom's thing, aren't we? The simulation thing?"

She sighed. "Believe me, the thought's occurred to me. It's very possible that my thinking is clouded. You know she's the reason I became a scientist."

I nodded.

"And look," she continued, "I know it's all circumstantial, I'm not crazy. It's just a series of descriptions of some kind of bizarre experience. But the *coincidence,* Gaspery, the way these moments seem to bleed into one another, I can't help but see it as some kind of evidence."

4

If we were living in a simulation, how would we know it was a simulation? I took the trolley home from the university at three in the morning. In the warm light of the moving car, I closed my eyes and marvelled at the detail. The gentle vibration of the trolley on its cushion of air. The sounds—the barely perceptible whisper of movement, the soft conversations here and there in the car, the tinny notes of a game escaping from a device somewhere. *We are living in a simulation,* I told myself, testing the idea, but it still seemed improbable to me, because I could smell the bouquet of yellow roses that the woman sitting beside me held carefully in both hands. *We are living in a simulation,* but I'm hungry and am I supposed to believe that that's a simulation too?

"I'm not saying these things add up to any kind of definite proof that we're living in a simulation," Zoey had said, an hour

ago in her office. "I'm saying I think there's enough here to jus-
tify an investigation."

How do you investigate reality? My hunger is a simulation,
I told myself, but I wanted a cheeseburger. Cheeseburgers are a
simulation. Beef is a simulation. (Actually, that was literally true.
Killing an animal for food would get you arrested both on Earth
and in the colonies.) I opened my eyes and thought, *The roses are
a simulation. The scent of roses is a simulation.*

"What would an investigation look like?" I'd asked her.

"I think you'd want to visit all those points in time," Zoey
said. "You'd want to speak with the letter writer in 1912, the
video artist in 2019 or 2020, and the novelist in 2203."

I remembered the news stories when time travel was invented
and then immediately made illegal outside of government facili-
ties. I remembered a chapter from a criminology textbook dedicated to the near-annihilating nightmare of the so-called Rose
Loop, when history had changed twenty-seven times before the
rogue traveller was taken out of commission and his damage
undone. I knew that one hundred forty-one of the two hundred
and five people serving life sentences on the moon were there
because they'd attempted time travel. It didn't matter if they'd
been successful or not; the attempt was enough to send you away
for life.

"Gaspery," Zoey had said, "I'm not sure why you look so
shocked. What does the sign on the building say?"

"Time Institute," I admitted.

She looked at me.

"I thought you were a physicist," I said.

"Well . . . yes," she said. There was a knowledge-and-achievement gap the size of the solar system in that pause between words. I heard that old kindness, that familiar sense that she was extending generosity toward me. We can't all be geniuses, I wanted to tell her, but we'd had that conversation when we were teenagers and it had gone poorly, so I didn't.

We are living in a simulation, I told myself as the trolley stopped a block from my apartment, but this fell so far short of, well, of the *reality,* for lack of a better word. I couldn't convince myself. I didn't believe it. There was a scheduled rainfall in— I glanced at my watch—two minutes. I stepped out of the trolley and walked very slowly, on purpose. I've always loved rain, and knowing that it isn't coming from clouds doesn't make me love it less.

5

In the weeks that followed, I tried to reacclimatize to the rhythms of my life. I rose at five in the afternoon in my tiny apartment, listened to music while I cooked, fed my cat, walked or took the trolley to work. I was at the hotel by seven p.m., gazing out at the lobby from behind dark glasses—most staffers didn't wear dark glasses, but as a light-sensitive native of the Night City who couldn't tolerate the diffuse glare of the dome, I had special dispensation from HR—and I stood there thinking of all of the things around me that might not be real. The stone of the lobby floor. The fabric of my clothes. My hands. My glasses. The footsteps of a woman crossing the lobby.

"Evening, Gaspery," the woman said.

"Talia. Hi."

"You were taking a very concentrated interest in the lobby floor."

"Can I ask you an extremely random question?"

"Please do," she said. "I've had a boring day."

"Do you ever catch yourself thinking about the simulation hypothesis?" It seemed worth asking. It was all I could think about.

She raised her eyebrows. "That's the idea that we're possibly living in a simulation, isn't it?"

"Yeah."

"Actually, yes. I have thought about it. I don't believe we're living in a simulation." Talia was gazing past me, past the lobby, to the street. "I don't know, maybe this is naïve of me, but I feel like a simulation should be better, you know? I mean, if you were going to the trouble to simulate that street, for example, couldn't all of the streetlights work?"

The streetlight across the street had been flickering for a number of weeks.

"I see your point."

"Well, anyway," Talia said, "good night."

"Good night." I returned to the exercise of noticing everything and telling myself that none of the things I noticed were real, but now I was distracted by her point. Something no one ever talked about in those days was the shabbiness of the moon colonies. I think we were all a little embarrassed by it.

"Yeah, I think it's fair to say the glamour's worn off," Zoey said when I saw her later that night. My shift ended at two a.m., so I'd called to ask if I could come over and see her. I'd known she'd be up—she'd never fully transitioned out of the Night City either, and, like me, she preferred to stay up all night—and she was taking a couple of days off work, so I took the trolley to her apartment. I'd been to this apartment only a handful of times, and had forgotten how dark it was. She'd painted the walls in a deep shade of grey. She had a collection of old-fashioned paper books—mostly history—and a framed painting on the wall that we'd made together when we were children. I was moved by it. We'd been about four and six, something like that, and we'd painted ourselves: a boy and a girl holding hands under a tree in exuberant colours.

"Where did the glamour go?" I asked. She'd poured me a generous glass of whisky, which I was sipping very slowly because I've never had much of an alcohol tolerance. She was already on her second drink.

"To the newer colonies, I suppose. Titan, I guess. Europa. The Far Colonies." We were at her kitchen table. She lived across the street from the Time Institute, which I'd known intellectually without fully absorbing. What did Zoey have? She'd been very close with our mother, and now that Mom was gone, what Zoey had was her work. Her work and almost nothing else, to all appearances, but who was I to judge. I leaned back in my chair, gazing over the Time Institute rooftops at the luminescent spires of beyond. Could I immigrate to the Far Colonies? Fantastical thought. But of course the thought that followed was *If we're living in a simulation, it's not like the Far Colonies are real either.*

"What happened to them?" I asked. "The letter writer back in the twentieth century, Edwin whatever his name was, and Olive Llewellyn?"

Zoey had somehow finished her second glass—I was still only halfway through my first—and poured herself a third.

"The letter writer went to war, returned home to England a broken man, and died in an insane asylum. Olive Llewellyn died on Earth. A pandemic broke out while she was on a book tour."

"Zoey," I said, "has your investigation started yet?"

"Sort of. Preliminary discussions are under way. The bureaucracy around travel is intense."

"Will you get to . . . Will you be the one to travel?"

"I almost left the Time Institute a few years ago," she said. "I agreed to stay on condition that I never have to travel again."

"You've travelled through *time*," I said, and my awe at my sister was boundless in that moment. "Where did you go?"

"I can't talk about it." Her expression was grim.

"Can you at least tell me why you don't want to do it anymore? I'd think it'd be . . ."

"You'd think it'd be interesting," she said. "It is. At first it's fascinating. It's a portal to a different world."

"Right, that's how I imagined it."

"But before you go, Gaspery, you might spend two years engaged in research. When you're going to a given point in time, you're there to investigate some specific thing, and you read up on everyone you expect to encounter. There are people at the Time Institute, hundreds of staff, whose entire job is researching long-dead people to compile dossiers for travellers, and your job is to study those dossiers until you know everything in them." She stopped to drink. "So, Gaspery, picture this scene. You step into a party, at some long-ago point in time, and you know exactly how and when each and every person in that room is going to die."

"That's pretty creepy," I admitted.

"And some of them are going to die in the most preventable ways, Gaspery. You might be talking to a woman, let's say she has young children, and you know she's going to drown at a picnic next Tuesday, and because you can't mess with the time line, the one thing you absolutely cannot say to her is 'Don't go swimming next week.' You have to let her die."

"You can't pull her from the water."

"Right."

For a while I wasn't sure what to say, so I gazed out the window at the rooftops and spires and wondered if letting someone die for the sake of the time line was something I could do. Zoey drank quietly.

"The job requires an almost inhuman level of detachment," she said finally. "Did I say *almost*? Not *almost* inhuman, *actually* inhuman."

"So someone will have to travel through time to investigate this," I said, "but it won't be you."

"It will be several people, but I don't know who. It's not exactly a popular job."

"Send me," I said. Because what I was thinking in that moment was that the theoretical woman who was going to drown next Tuesday was going to drown anyway.

She looked at me, surprised. Two spots of pink had appeared on her cheeks, but otherwise she seemed perfectly sober.

"Absolutely not."

"Why not?"

"One, it's a horrifically dangerous job. Two, you're not qualified."

"What kind of background would you have to have, to travel back in time and talk to people? That's what it is, isn't it? I mean, what are the qualifications?"

"There's a barrage of psychological testing, followed by years of training."

"I could do that," I said. "I could go back to school, I could do whatever training was required. You know I almost finished my criminology degree. I know how to conduct an interview."

She was quiet.

"You want to keep the circle small here," I said, "don't you? Imagine the panic if word got out that we're living in a simulation."

"We don't know that we're living in a simulation, and I don't know that *panic* is quite the word. More like terminal ennui."

I decided to look up *ennui* later. There are words you encounter all your life without knowing what they mean.

"Zoey," I said, "I'm not doing anything with my life."

"Don't say that," she said, too quickly.

"This is just . . . this situation," I said, "this thing, whatever it is, this possibility I guess, it's the most interested I've been about anything in maybe my entire life."

"Then get a hobby, Gaspery. Take up calligraphy or archery or something."

"Can you just think about it, Zoey? Talk to whoever you have to talk to? Can I be considered? If we're talking about travelling through time here, then there's no real rush, is there? I'd have time to prepare, I could do whatever you want, go back to school, psychological training, whatever—" I realized I was babbling, so I stopped.

"No," she said. "Absolutely not." She drained her glass. "When I say it's a dangerous job, Gaspery, I mean I wouldn't want anyone I love to do it."

6

I didn't see Zoey again for three weeks after that, and there was an away message on her device. I went to work, I came home from work, I paced my apartment and talked to the cat. Finally, on a day off from the hotel, I left her a voicemail to say I was coming to her office. She didn't respond, but I boarded a trolley to the Time Institute in the late afternoon. She'd told me her schedule. I knew she'd be there. I watched the pale streets slipping past, the old stone buildings with missing pieces of masonry and the ramshackle illegal dwellings pressed close against them—the influence of the Night City seeping in, a whiff of disorder that I found invigorating—and I had a strange, wild notion that she might be dead. She worked too much and drank too much. In that first year after our mother died, my thoughts often veered toward disaster.

I stood outside the Time Institute, white stone monolith, and called her one more time. Nothing. It was around six o'clock. A few people emerged from the building, singly or in pairs. I found myself studying their faces, wondering what it might be like to have a job with stakes attached to it, and then one of the faces was Ephrem's.

"Eph," I said.

He looked up, startled.

"Gaspery! What are you doing here?"

I'd talked to Ephrem at my mother's funeral, briefly, but that day was a blur. We hadn't spoken at any length since the last dinner party I'd attended at his house, a year ago now. Perhaps it was just the dome lighting—dimming gently but also increasingly silvery, in a rough approximation of an Earth twilight—but Ephrem looked older than I remembered, older and more careworn.

"I was about to ask you the same thing," I said. "What's an arborist doing at the Time Institute?" He hesitated, and in that beat, I saw an opening. There was something he didn't want to tell me, and there was something I wasn't supposed to know. "You work here, don't you?"

He nodded. "Yes. For some time now."

"Then do you know about the project Zoey's working on? The simulation thing?"

"For god's sake, Gaspery, don't say another word." Ephrem was smiling, but I could tell he meant it. "It's been a while. Shall we grab a cup of tea?"

"Love to."

"Come see my office," he said. "I'll get some tea sent up."

We walked together in silence through the atrium, past Security, into an elevator and through successive white corridors that all looked the same to me, a maze of blank doors and opaque glass.

"Here we are," he said.

His office was identical to Zoey's but had a bonsai tree in the window. A tea service was waiting for us on the table, with three cups. I'd known Ephrem half my life, but had I ever really asked him about his work? He'd told me he was an arborist, I'd asked him the occasional question about a tree, but apparently I knew much less about my friend than I'd thought. His office was on a high floor, overlooking the spires of Colony One. In the distance, I saw the Grand Luna Hotel.

"How long have you been here?" I asked.

"About a decade." He was pouring tea, but he paused for a moment, considering. "No, seven years. It only feels like a decade."

"I thought you were an arborist."

"I miss that job, to be honest. I'm afraid trees are just a hobby now. Will you join me?"

I moved over to his meeting table, which was exactly like Zoey's. I was overcome by the strangeness of the moment, the disorienting sense of one reality slipping away and being replaced by another. *But I've known you for years,* I wanted to say, *and you're an arborist, not a suit at the Time Institute. We graduated high school together.*

"Were trees easier?" I asked.

"Than my current job? Yes. Very much so." His device vibrated. He glanced at the screen and winced.

"Why didn't you tell me you worked here?"

"It's just . . . it's awkward," he said. "By *awkward,* I mean classified. The thing is, I can't really answer questions about my job, so I don't like to talk about it."

"Must be strange," I said, "doing something secret." By *strange,* I meant wonderful.

"I try not to lie about it. If you'd asked where I was working, I'd have said I was doing some work with the Time Institute, and let you assume it was somehow tree-related."

"Okay," I said. The silence extended around us. I didn't know how to ask for what I wanted. *Hire me, let me in, let me be a part of whatever it is you people are doing here.* "Ephrem," I began, but the door opened just then, and Zoey came in. Her expression was set in a way I hadn't seen since childhood. Zoey was furious. She sat across from me, ignored her tea, and stared into my eyes until I was forced to look away.

"I've been losing staring contests with my sister since I was five," I said to Ephrem. "Maybe four." He rewarded me with a weak smile. No one spoke. My gaze drifted back to the bonsai tree.

Finally, mercifully, Ephrem cleared his throat.

"Listen," he said. "No one's broken any rules here. When

Zoey spoke with you about the anomaly, Gaspery, it hadn't been classified yet."

Zoey looked at her tea.

"Of course," Ephrem said, "that doesn't mean you should be standing outside the Time Institute repeating the things she told you."

"I'm sorry," I said. "Ephrem, can I ask, is it real?"

"What do you mean?"

"The things Zoey told me about seemed like a pattern, but, well, it was our mom's thing," I said. "Simulation hypothesis."

"I remember her talking about it," he said gently.

"I think that when you lose someone, it's easy to see patterns that aren't there."

Ephrem nodded. "True. I don't know if there's anything there," he said. "But I wasn't close with your mother, which makes me a somewhat neutral party in this question, and I think there's enough to make it worth investigating."

"Can I help?" I asked.

"*No,*" Zoey muttered, barely audible.

"Zoey did tell me that you wanted to work here." I noticed that Ephrem was very carefully not looking at Zoey.

"Yes," I said, "I would."

"*Gaspery,*" Zoey said.

"Why do you want to work here?" Ephrem asked.

"Because it's interesting," I said. "I'm more interested in this than—well, than anything I can remember, honestly. I hope that doesn't make me seem desperate."

"Not at all," Ephrem said. "It just makes you sound interested. All of us are interested, or we wouldn't be here. Do you know what we do here?"

"Not really," I said.

"We safeguard the integrity of our time line," he said. "We investigate anomalies."

"Have there been others?"

"Usually it turns out to be nothing," Ephrem said. "My first case at the Institute involved a doppelgänger. According to our best facial-recognition software, the same woman appeared in photographs and video footage taken in 1925 and 2093. I was able to collect DNA and establish that they were two different women."

"You said *usually*," I said.

"On a few occasions," Ephrem said, "we haven't been able to make a determination one way or the other." I could tell he was unsettled by this.

"Is there something you're looking for?" I asked.

"There are several things we're looking for." He was quiet for a moment. "The aspect of our work that relates to the anomaly," he said, "is a continuing investigation into whether we're living in a simulation."

"Do you think we are?"

"There's a faction," he said carefully, "myself among them, that believes time travel works better than it should."

"What do you mean?"

"I mean that there are fewer loops than one might reasonably expect. I mean that sometimes we change the time line and then the time line seems to *repair* itself, in a way that doesn't make sense to me. The course of history should be irrevocably altered every single time we travel back in the time line, but, well, it isn't. Sometimes events seemingly change to accommodate the time traveller's interference, so that a generation later it's as if the traveller were never there."

"None of which is proof of a simulation," Zoey said quickly.

"Right. For obvious reasons," Ephrem said, "it's difficult to confirm."

"But you could move a step closer to confirmation by identifying a glitch in the simulation," I said.

"Yes, exactly."

"Gaspery," Zoey said, "I know it's interesting, but it's a troubling line of work."

"Zoey and I have some disagreements regarding the Time Institute," Ephrem said. "I think it's fair to say that our experiences here have been different."

"Yeah, that's fair," Zoey said flatly.

"But what I can tell you," Ephrem said, "is that it's an interesting place to work."

"What *I* can tell you," Zoey said, "is that Ephrem missed his recruitment goals this year, last year, and the year before."

"The training and the job both require immense discretion," Ephrem said, ignoring her, "and a great deal of focus."

"I can focus," I said. "I can be discreet."

"Well," Ephrem said, "I'll set up a screening interview for you."

"Thank you," I said. "This will sound . . . look, I don't mean to sound pathetic, but I've literally never had an interesting job before."

Ephrem smiled. "I'm not worried about the screening interview. You'll pass easily. This calls for a celebration."

But if it called for a celebration, why was my sister speaking so little, why did she look so grim? *A troubling line of work.* Look, I wanted to tell her, as Ephrem ordered three glasses of champagne, I would rather do a dangerous job than a job that makes me comatose with boredom, but I was afraid if I said this she might start to cry.

7

A week later I arrived at the hotel fifteen minutes before my shift, and went to Talia's office.

"Gaspery," she said.

I started to close the door, but she shook her head and rose from behind her desk. "Let's go for a walk."

"I only have a few—"

"You know, it's interesting." She gestured for me to walk out ahead of her. "I studied the history of work in university, and if there's one historical constant over the centuries, it's that no one especially wants to mess with HR." She opened the side door and we emerged into daylight by the loading dock. "I told your supervisor that I needed to meet with you. No one will mind."

Today's weather programming called for clouds, so the daylight was dim and greyish. I found it unsettling.

"It's hard to get used to," Talia said. She'd seen me glance uneasily at the sky. We were walking toward the path that ran alongside the Colony One river. All three colonies had rivers, for mental health reasons, running along identical white stone riverbeds, with identical white stone bridges arcing across them. They were engineering marvels. They all sounded exactly the same. "Why did you leave the Night City?" she asked.

"Bad divorce," I said. "I just wanted a fresh start." There was comfort in the sameness of the river sound; if I didn't look up, if I didn't pay attention to the strange greyish fake-cloudy-day light, I could pretend I was home. "Why did you come here?"

"I'm from here," she said. "I didn't move to the Night City till I was nine."

"Oh."

We were approaching a bridge. In the Night City, the bridge would've had a selection of derelicts napping or getting high underneath, in the peace and shadows of the embankment, but here there was just an old man on a bench, sitting alone and staring at the water.

"You came to my office to give your notice," Talia said.

"How did you know?"

"Because my boss's boss's boss told me to speak with a couple of suits from the Time Institute three days ago. I could tell from their questions that they were vetting you for a position."

Is there an unease that's specific to the sense of an invisible bureaucracy in motion around you? Talia stopped walking, so I stopped too, and I gazed down at the water. When I was a kid I used to float little boats down the Night City river, but the Night City river was a dark and sparkling thing, reflecting both sunlight and the blackness of space. The Colony One river was pale and milky, reflecting the fake clouds on the dome.

"We used to live there," Talia said, pointing, and I looked up and across the river at one of the oldest and most splendid of the grand apartment buildings, a white cylinder of a tower with a garden on every balcony. "My parents worked for the Time Institute."

I wasn't sure what to say. There was no non-catastrophic reason I could think of why a family would go from one of the most fashionable addresses in Colony One to a falling-down house in the Night City.

"They were both travellers," Talia said. "Until a mission went wrong in some kind of awful way, after which my parents were unable to work, and within a year we were in that run-down neighbourhood in the Night City."

"I'm sorry." I resented having to say this, because the thing was, I loved the Night City, and that run-down neighbourhood was my home. My family—me, Zoey, our mom—weren't there because we *had* to be there, we were there because in my mother's words, "at least this place has some character to it, not like those sterile colonies with the fake lighting," although as I remembered this, I was also remembering that we couldn't afford to fix the roof when it leaked.

Talia was looking at me. "Drunks are indiscreet," she said.

"As I'm sure you're aware, if you've ever thought about the question for more than five minutes, sending someone back in time inevitably changes history. *The traveller's presence itself is a disruption,* that's the phrase I remember my dad using. There's no way to go back, engage with the past, and leave the time line perfectly unchanged."

"Right," I said. I wasn't sure what she was getting at, but listening to her made me so uneasy that I couldn't meet her eyes.

"Sometimes the Time Institute goes back in time and undoes the damage, ensures that the traveller doesn't do the thing that changes history. You know, the little thing, like you hold open the door for the woman who goes on to create a civilization-ending algorithm or whatever. Sometimes they go back and undo the damage, but not always. Do you want to know how they make that decision?"

"That sounds extremely classified," I said.

"Oh, it *is,* Gaspery, but I like you and also I've developed a reckless streak in my old age, so I'm going to tell you anyway." (She was, what, thirty-five? In that moment, I found her thrillingly jaded.) "Here's the metric: they only go back and undo the damage *if the damage affects the Time Institute.* What am I, Gaspery? How would you describe me?"

This felt like a trap. "I . . ."

"It's okay," she said, "you can say it. I'm a bureaucrat. HR is bureaucracy."

"Okay."

"As is the Time Institute. The premier research university on the moon, possessor of the only working time machine in existence, intimately enmeshed in government and in law enforcement. Even *one* of those things would imply a formidable bureaucracy, don't you think? What you have to understand is that bureaucracy is an organism, and the prime goal of every organism is self-protection. Bureaucracy exists to protect itself." She was gazing across the river again. "We lived on the third floor," she said, pointing. "The balcony with the vines and rose-bushes."

"It's nice," I said.

"Isn't it? Look, I understand why you'd want to work with the Time Institute," she said. "It must seem like an exciting opportunity. It's not like you've got much of a career path at the hotel. But just know that when the Institute is done with you, they'll throw you away." She spoke so casually that I wasn't sure if I'd heard her correctly. "I have a meeting," she said. "You should probably start your shift in the next hour or so." She turned and left me there.

I looked back at the apartment building. I'd been to one of those apartments once, years ago, for a party, and I'd been fairly drunk at the time, but I remembered vaulted ceilings and spacious rooms. What I was thinking was that if anything went wrong with the Time Institute, I would never be able to say I hadn't been warned.

But I felt such impatience with my life. I turned back to the hotel, and found that I couldn't go in. The hotel was the past. I wanted the future. I called Ephrem.

"Could I start early?" I asked. "I know the plan was to give the hotel two weeks' notice, but could I just start the training now? Tonight?"

"Sure," he said. "Could you be here in an hour?"

8

"Would you like some tea?" Ephrem asked.

"Please."

He typed something into his device, and we sat together at the meeting table. A sudden memory: drinking chai tea with Ephrem and Ephrem's mother after school one day at Ephrem's apartment, which was nicer than mine. Ephrem's mother had a job she could do from home, I remembered; she'd been staring at a screen. Ephrem and I were both studying, so it must have been just before an exam, during a period when I'd been experimenting with (a) tea and (b) being a good student. I was about to bring up this moment—*Do you remember?*—when there was a soft chime at the door, and a young man came in with a tray, which he left on the table with a nod. *Chai tea is real,* I told myself, and then I realized: Ephrem must remember that long-ago moment too, because he'd only ever served me chai when I'd come here.

"Here you are." Ephrem passed me a steaming mug.

"Why didn't Zoey want me to work here?"

He sighed. "She had a bad experience a few years back. I don't know the details."

"Yes, you do."

"Yes, I do. Look, this is just a rumour, but I heard she was in love with a traveller, then the traveller went rogue and got lost in time. That's literally all I know."

"No, it isn't."

"Literally all I know that isn't classified," Ephrem said.

"How do you get lost in time?"

"Suppose you were to intentionally fuck with the time line. The Time Institute might decide not to bring you back to the present."

"Why would anyone intentionally fuck with the time line?"

"Exactly," Ephrem said. "Don't do that, and you'll be fine." He leaned over to touch a console on the wall, and a time line with photographs of people was suspended in the air between us. "I've been working on an investigation plan for you," he said. "We don't want to place you in the centre of the anomaly, because we don't know what the anomaly is, or how dangerous it might be. We want you to interview people who we think have seen it."

He enlarged a very old photograph, black-and-white, of a worried-looking young man in military uniform. "This is Edwin

St. Andrew, who experienced something in the forest at Caiette. You'll visit him, and see if he'll talk about it."

"I didn't know he was a soldier." .

"He won't be when you speak with him. You'll talk to him in 1912, and then later he'll go on to have a very bad time on the Western Front. More tea?"

"Thank you." I had no idea what the Western Front was and hoped it would be covered in my training.

He swiped the time line to the side, and I was looking at the composer from the footage Zoey had shown me. "In January 2020," Ephrem continued, "an artist named Paul James Smith gave a performance that involved a video, and it seems like that video maybe shows the anomaly that St. Andrew described a century earlier, but we don't know where exactly that video was taken. We don't have complete footage of his concert, just the clip Zoey showed you. You'll speak to him and see what you can learn."

Ephrem swiped again, and I saw another photograph, an old man playing a violin in an airship terminal, his eyes closed. "This is Alan Sami," Ephrem said. "He played the violin for several years in the Oklahoma City Airship Terminal, circa 2200, and we believe it's his music that Olive Llewellyn references in *Marienbad*. You'll interview him and find out more about the music. Really just find out anything you can." He moved on through the time line, and there was Olive Llewellyn, my mother's favourite author, long-ago resident of Talia Anderson's childhood home. "And here's Olive Llewellyn. I regret to report that absolutely no one keeps surveillance footage for two hundred years, so there's no record of whatever Olive Llewellyn may or may not have experienced there prior to writing *Marienbad*. You'll interview her on her last book tour."

"When was her last book tour?" I asked.

"November 2203. Early days of the SARS Twelve pandemic. Don't worry, you won't get sick."

"I've never heard of it."

"It was one of our childhood immunizations," Ephrem said.

"Will there be other investigators assigned to the case?"

"Several. They'll look at different angles, interview different people, or interview the same people in a different way. You may meet some of them, but if they're good at their jobs, you'll never know who they are. From your perspective, Gaspery, this is not a complicated assignment. You'll conduct a few interviews, and then hand off your findings to a more senior investigator, who will take over and make the final determination, and if all goes well, there will be other investigations for you. You could have an interesting career here." He was gazing at the time line. "Where I think you'll start," he said, "is by interviewing the violinist."

"Okay," I said. "When do I talk to him?"

"In about five years," Ephrem said. "You have some training to do first."

9

The training wasn't like immersing myself in a different world. It was like immersing myself in successive different worlds, these moments that had arisen one after another after another, worlds fading out so gradually that their loss was apparent only in retrospect. Years of private instruction in small rooms in the Institute, years of passing by people who may or may not have been my fellow students in the halls—no one wore name tags here—and years of studying quietly in the Time Institute library, or in my apartment late at night with my cat asleep on my lap. Five years after I left the hotel, I reported for the first time to the travel chamber.

It was a midsize room made entirely of some kind of composite stone. At one end was a bench, moulded into a deep indentation in the wall. The bench faced an extremely ordinary-looking desk. Zoey was waiting there, with a device that looked unnervingly like a gun.

"I'm going to shoot a tracker into your arm," she said.

"Good morning, Zoey. I'm fine, thanks for asking. Nice to see you too."

"It's a microcomputer. It interacts with your device, which interacts with the machine."

"Okay," I said, giving up on pleasantries. "So the tracker sends information to my device?"

"Remember that time I gave you a cat?" she said.

"Of course. Marvin. He's napping at home as we speak."

"We sent an agent back to another century," Zoey said, "but the agent fell in love with someone and didn't want to come home, so she removed her own tracker, fed it to a cat, and then when we tried to forcibly return her to the present, the cat appeared in the travel chamber instead of her."

"Wait," I said, "my cat's from another century?"

"Your cat's from 1985," she said.

"What," I said, at a loss for words.

She took my hand—when was the last time we'd touched one another?—and I observed her grim concentration as she shot a silver pellet into my left arm. It hurt much more than I would've imagined. She opened a projection over the desk, and turned her attention to the floating screen.

"You should have told me," I said. "You should have told me my cat was a time traveller."

"Honestly, Gaspery, what difference would it make. A cat's a cat."

"You never were an animal person, were you."

Her mouth was set in a thin line. She wouldn't look at me.

"You should be happy for me," I said, while she was adjusting something in her projection. "This is the only thing I've ever really wanted to do, and I'm doing it."

"Oh, Gaspery," she said absently. "My poor little lamb. Device?"

"Here."

She took my device, held it close to the projection, and handed it back to me.

"Okay," she said. "Your first destination has been programmed. Go sit in the machine."

10

A transcript:

Gaspery Roberts: Okay, it's on. Thank you for taking the time to speak with me.

Alan Sami: You're welcome. Thank you for lunch.

GR: Now, just for the benefit of my recording, you're a violinist.

AS: I am. I play in the airship terminal.

GR: For spare change?

AS: For pleasure. I don't need the money, to be clear.

GR: But you do collect change, in that hat at your feet . . .

AS: Well, people were throwing change at me, so I did at one point decide to just turn my hat upside down in front of me, so that all the change would at least land in one place.

GR: May I ask, why do you do it, if you don't need the money?

AS: Well, because I love it, son. I love playing the violin, and I love seeing people.

GR: I'd like to play a short clip for you, if I may.

AS: Of music?

GR: Music with some ambient noises. I'll play it, and then I'm going to ask you to tell me anything you can about it. That sound all right?

AS: Sure. Go ahead.

[. . .]

GR: That was you, right?

AS: Yes, that's me in the airship terminal. Poor-quality recording, though.

GR: How can you be sure it's you?

AS: How can I . . . really? Well, son, because I know the music and I heard an airship. That *whoosh* just at the end.

GR: Let's focus on the music for a moment. That piece you were playing, can you tell me about it?

AS: My lullaby. I composed it, but I never gave it a title. It was something I made up for my wife, my late wife.

GR: Your late . . . I'm sorry.

AS: Thank you.

GR: Is there—did you ever record yourself playing it, or write down the score?

AS: Neither. Why?

GR: Well, as I mentioned, I'm an assistant to a music historian. I've been tasked with investigating similarities and differences between the music played at airship terminals in various regions on Earth.

AS: And your affiliation, what institution was that, again?

GR: University of British Columbia.

AS: That where your accent's from?

GR: My accent?

AS: It just shifted. I have an ear for accents.

GR: Oh. I'm from Colony Two.

AS: Interesting. My wife was from Colony One, but I wouldn't say she sounded anything like you. How long have you been doing this?

GR: Assisting in investigations? A few years.

AS: You go to school for that? How does a person get into that line of work?

GR: Fair question. I was spinning my wheels, if we're being honest here. I had a job in hotel security. It was fine. I just stood around a hotel lobby, staring at people. But then, well, I saw an opportunity. Something came up that really interested me, in a way I'd never been interested in anything. I spent five years in training, studying linguistics and psychology and history.

AS: I understand the history part, but why psychology and linguistics?

GR: Well, linguistics because people speak differently, at different points in history, and if you're dealing with old music that has a spoken-word element, it's helpful.

AS: Makes sense. And psychology?

GR: Personal interest. It wasn't relevant. It wasn't relevant at all. I don't know why I mentioned it.

AS: Methinks the lady doth protest too much.

GR: Wait, did you just call me a lady?

AS: That was Shakespeare, son. Come on, now. Didn't you go to school?

11

"Smooth," Zoey said when she reviewed the recording. "Real sophisticate there."

Ephrem, who was sitting with us in her office, suppressed a smile.

"I know," I said. "Sorry."

"No, look," my sister said, "we didn't cover Shakespeare in your training."

"Zoey," I said, "Ephrem, what would happen, just theoretically, if I messed up?"

"Don't mess up." Ephrem glanced at his device. "I'm sorry," he said, "I have a meeting with my boss, but I'll see you in my office in an hour." He left us then, and I was alone with my sister.

"What were your impressions of the violinist?" Zoey asked.

"He was in his eighties," I said, "maybe even nineties. He had a slow way of talking, like his accent kind of dragged everything out. He'd done that thing to his eyes, that colour-change thing? His eyes were this strange shade of purple. Violet, I guess."

"Probably all the rage in his youth."

She looked back at the transcript, rereading something. I rose and went to the window. It was night, and the dome had gone clear. Earth was rising on the horizon, a vision in green and blue.

"Zoey," I said, "can I ask you something?"

"Of course."

I turned back to her, and she looked up from the transcript.

"Do you remember Talia Anderson from the Night City?" I asked.

"No. No, I don't think so."

"She was in my grade for a while in elementary school. Her family lived in the Olive Llewellyn house, and then I ran into her again when she hired me for that hotel security job."

"Wait," Zoey said, "are we talking about Natalia Anderson at the Grand Luna Hotel?"

"Yes."

Zoey nodded. "She was on the list of people we interviewed when you were being cleared for this position."

"How do you remember a name on a list from five years ago?"

"I don't know," she said. "I just do."

"I wish I had your brain. Anyway. She kind of warned me off coming here, to be honest."

"So did I," Zoey said.

"I guess her parents worked here," I said, ignoring this. "A long time ago. She said her dad was indiscreet."

Zoey was watching me closely. "What did she say?"

"She said, *The traveller's presence itself is a disruption*—"

"Those exact words?"

"I think so. Why?"

"That's from a classified training manual that went out of circulation ten years ago. I wonder if she's telling anyone else about it. What else did she say?"

"She said that when the Institute was done with me, it would throw me away."

Zoey looked away. "It's not always the easiest place to work," she said. "Staff turnover is high. You'll remember that I tried to dissuade you."

"You were afraid I'd get thrown away?"

She was quiet for so long that I thought she wasn't going to answer. When she spoke again, she wouldn't look at me, and her voice was strained. "I was close with someone, a long time ago, another traveller who was investigating something else. She messed up."

"What happened to her?"

Her hand drifted to the necklace she always wore. It was a simple gold chain, and I'd never really noticed it before, but from the way she touched it, I understood that the lost traveller had given it to her.

"Here's what you have to understand," she said. "You don't have to be a terrible person to intentionally try to change the time line. You just have to have a moment of weakness. Really just a moment. When I say *weakness,* I might mean something more like *humanity.*"

"And if you intentionally change the time line . . ."

"It's not difficult to deliberately lose someone in time. Frame them for a crime they didn't commit, for example, or, in less serious cases, they can just be placed somewhere with no way home."

"Wouldn't framing a traveller for a crime have, well, some repercussions for the time line?"

"The Research department maintains a list of crimes," Zoey said. "Carefully selected, carefully vetted to avoid any major repercussions."

(*"Bureaucracy exists to protect itself," Talia said, gazing out over the river.*)

Zoey cleared her throat. "Big day tomorrow," she said. "Remind me where you're going first?"

"1912," I said, "to talk to Edwin St. Andrew. I'm going to pretend to be a priest and see if he'll talk to me in the church."

"Right. And then?"

"Then I'm going to January 2020," I said, "to talk to the video artist, Paul James Smith, see what we can learn about that weird footage."

She nodded. "And you talk to Olive Llewellyn the next day?"

"Yeah." By now I'd read all of her books. I hadn't especially liked any of them, but it was hard to parse whether this was the fault of the books or the fault of the dread I felt when I thought of her, given the timing of the scheduled interview.

"You know you're meeting her in the last week of her life," Zoey said. "You'll interview her in Philadelphia, and she'll die three days later in a hotel room in New York."

"I know." I felt a little sick about it.

Zoey's face softened. "Remember how Mom used to quote *Marienbad* at us when we were kids?"

I nodded, and for a moment I was transported back to the hospital, the last days of our mother, the week outside of time and space when we never left her side.

"But you'll keep it together, right?" In the way my sister looked at me, I knew she saw a previous Gaspery, a shiftless version of myself who was prone to error, who lived aimlessly and hadn't spent the past five years in training and study and research.

"Of course. I'm a professional."

I knew the facts of the life, and of the death: Olive Llewellyn died in a pandemic that began during a book tour. She died in an Atlantic Republic hotel room. But of course the thought of breaking the protocol occurred to me, then and in the morning two days later when I reported to the travel chamber, when the coordinates were entered into my device, when I stepped into the machine to meet her.

Last Book Tour on Earth /

2203

"LISTEN," THE JOURNALIST SAID, "I DON'T MEAN TO MAKE you uncomfortable or put you on the spot. But I'm curious if you experienced something strange in the Oklahoma City Airship Terminal."

In the quiet, Olive could hear the soft hum of the building, the sounds of ventilation and plumbing. Perhaps she wouldn't have admitted it if he hadn't caught her toward the end of the tour, if she hadn't been so tired. The journalist, Gaspery-Jacques Roberts, was watching her closely. She felt he already knew what she was about to say.

"I don't mind talking about this," she said, "but I'm afraid I'll seem too eccentric if it makes it into the final version of the interview. Could we go off the record for a moment?"

"Yes," he said.

"I was in the terminal. I was walking toward my flight, and I remember I walked by a guy playing a violin. And then all of a sudden, everything went dark and I was in a forest. Just for a second. It was . . ."

"It was exactly like you described it in the book," Gaspery said.

"Yes."

"Can you tell me anything else?"

"There's not much else. It was so fast. I had an impression . . . This is going to sound crazy, but I was in two places at once. When I say I was in a forest, I was also still in the terminal."

"I knew it," he said.

"I'm not sure . . ." Olive didn't know how to ask the question. "Does it mean something?" she asked.

He looked at her, and seemed to grapple with what to say next. "This will sound silly," he said, in tones of forced lightness, "but my editor over at *Contingencies Magazine* likes me to end interviews with a fun question."

Olive clenched her hands together and nodded.

"Okay, so," he said, "this is kind of a question about destiny, I guess?" Olive noticed that he was sweating. "Barring some kind of unforeseen catastrophe, assuming that our technology continues to advance, we'll probably have time travel in the next century. If a time traveller appeared before you and told you to drop everything and go home immediately, would you do it?"

"How would I know they were a time traveller?"

The door was opening, and Olive's publicist was coming in.

"Well, let's say there was something about the person that couldn't be reconciled."

"For example."

Gaspery leaned forward, speaking softly and quickly. "Well, for example, suppose this person were an adult," he said. "Now suppose this person, this adult in his thirties, had a name you'd made up for a book that you only published five years ago."

"How's it going in here?" Aretta asked.

"Great," Gaspery said. "Your timing's perfect."

"You could've changed your name," Olive said.

"I could have." He held her gaze. "But I didn't." His tone brightened as he rose. "Olive, thanks so much for your time. Especially that last question. I know fun questions are the worst."

"Olive, you look tired," Aretta said. "You doing okay?"

"Just tired," Olive said, parroting the explanation.

"But you're going home right after this, aren't you?" Gaspery said smoothly. "Straight from here to the airship terminal, right? Well, anyway, goodbye, thank you!"

"No, she has another— Oh," Aretta said, "yes, goodbye!" Gaspery was gone. "He's a little odd, isn't he?"

"A little," Olive said.

"What was that about going home? You have another three days on Earth."

"Something's come up."

She frowned. "But—"

But Olive had never been more certain of anything. She'd never been warned more clearly in her life. "I'm sorry," she said, "I know this causes problems for everyone, but I need to go to the airship terminal. I'm going home on the next flight."

"What?"

"Aretta," Olive said, "you should go home to your family."

It's shocking to wake up in one world and find yourself in another by nightfall, but the situation isn't actually all that unusual. You wake up married, then your spouse dies over the course of the day; you wake in peacetime and by noon your country is at war; you wake in ignorance and by evening it's clear that a pandemic is already here. You wake on a book tour with several days left to go, and by evening you're racing toward home, your suitcase abandoned in a hotel room.

Olive called her husband from the car. It was a self-driven car, for which she was grateful; there was no driver to hear her and wonder if she'd lost her mind, which was something she was wondering herself. "Dion," she said, "I'm going to ask you to do something that's going to sound kind of extreme."

"Okay," he said.

"We need to pull Sylvie out of school."

"Like, not bring her in tomorrow? I have to work."

"Could you go and pick her up now?"

"Olive, what's this about?"

Outside the window, the Philadelphia suburbs were a blur of apartment towers. You can have an excellent marriage and still be unable to tell your spouse absolutely everything. "It's about this new virus," Olive said. "I met someone at the hotel with some inside knowledge."

"What kind of inside knowledge?"

"It's bad, Dion, it's spreading out of control."

"In the colonies too?"

"How many flights are there every day between Earth and the moon?"

He drew in his breath. "Okay," he said. "Okay. I'll go get her."

"Thank you. I'm on my way home."

"What? I know it's serious if you're cutting a book tour short."

"It's serious, Dion, it seems like it's really serious," and Olive realized she was beginning to cry.

"Don't cry," he said softly. "Don't cry. I'm heading to the school now. I'll bring her home."

In the departure lounge, Olive found a corner far from anyone else and took out her device. There was no new news of the pandemic, but she ordered three months' worth of pharmaceutical supplies, then bottled water for good measure, then a mountain of new toys for Sylvie. By the time she boarded the flight she had spent a small fortune and felt mildly insane.

What it was like to leave Earth:

A rapid ascent over the green-and-blue world, then the world was blotted out all at once by clouds. The atmosphere turned thin and blue, the blue shaded into indigo, and then—it was like slipping through the skin of a bubble—there was black space. Six hours to the moon. Olive had bought a package of surgical masks at the airport—sold to travellers who'd picked up colds on the road—and she was wearing three of them, which made it difficult to breathe. She had a window seat and was all but curled around her armrest, trying to stay as far from other people as possible. The surface of the moon rose out of blackness, bright from a distance and grey up close, the opaque bubbles of Colonies One, Two, and Three gleaming in the sunlight.

Her device lit up with a soft chime. She frowned at the new

appointment alert, because she couldn't remember having scheduled a doctor's appointment, and then she understood: Dion had scheduled the appointment for her. He'd seen how much money she'd just spent on canned goods. He thought she was losing her grip.

Then the landing, so gentle after that hurtling speed between Earth and the moon. Olive put on dark glasses to hide her tears. But it wasn't unreasonable, actually, the doctor's appointment. If Dion had called from a business trip to say that a plague was coming and she should pull their child out of school, if she'd seen those massive charges go through on their shared credit account, she would've feared for his sanity too. She waited as long as possible before disembarking, in order to create some distance between herself and other people, and stayed as far away as possible from everyone in the spaceport and on the platform for the Colony Two train. In the train car she stared out the window at the passing tunnel lights, through the composite glass to the moon's bright surface. She disembarked on a platform, where she kept reaching for her suitcase and then remembering that she was never going to see it again.

Olive had a moment of passing regret for the strange starweapon burrs that she'd pulled from her socks in the Republic of Texas—she'd looked forward to showing them to Sylvie—but beyond that there was nothing of any real value in that suitcase, she told herself. (But she felt bereft: she'd been travelling with the suitcase for years now and it was almost a friend.) The trolley arrived. Olive sat close to the doors, for increased airflow—it was all coming back to her now, all of her research into pandemics—and the trolley glided through the streets and boulevards of this city of white stone, which had never looked more beautiful to her. The bridges arching over the street were possessed of uncommon architectural grace; the trees lining the boulevards and softening the tower balconies were almost unnaturally verdant, oversaturated in their green; and then there were the countless little shops with people walking in and out—unmasked, ungloved, oblivious, blind to the imminent catastrophe—and the sight of them was too much, actually, she could bear no more but of course she had to. Olive was weeping quietly, so no one came near her.

She disembarked early, and walked the last ten blocks in the sunlight. The Colony Two dome was displaying her favourite kind of sky, white skittering clouds on a background of deep blue. What was missing was the sound of suitcase wheels on cobblestones.

Olive turned the corner and there was the complex where she lived, a line of square white buildings with staircases leading down from the second and third floors to the sidewalk. She took the stairs to the second floor with a sense of unreality. How could she be home so soon? Without her suitcase? And why, because a journalist had said something strange about time travel? She raised her hand to knock—her keys were in her suitcase, on Earth—but froze. What if the contagion were on her clothes? She took off her jacket, her shoes, and then—after only a moment of hesitation—her pants and shirt. She looked down at the street and a passerby looked quickly away.

She called Dion.

"Olive, where are you?"

"Could you unlock the door, and then take Sylvie into the bedroom, and stay in there till I come into the room?"

"Olive . . ."

"I'm afraid of the contagion," Olive said. "I'm outside the front door, but I want to take a shower before either of you hug me. It could be on my clothes." Her clothes were puddled around her feet.

"Olive," he said, and she heard the pain in his voice. He thought she was terribly, desperately unwell, but not from the approaching pandemic.

"Please."

"Okay," he said. "I'll do it."

The lock clicked open. Olive waited for a slow count of ten, then let herself in, dropped her device and underwear into a heap on the floor, and went straight to the shower room. She scrubbed herself with soap, then found the cleaning alcohol, retraced her footsteps, and disinfected every surface she'd touched, then turned on the air purifier to its highest setting and opened all the windows, then used her towel to lift her underwear from the floor and dropped both underwear and towel into the garbage disposal, then disinfected her device, then disinfected the floor where the device had been, then disinfected her hands again.

This will be our lives now, she thought dully, *memorizing which surfaces we've touched.* Olive took a deep breath, and arranged her face into a semblance of calm. She opened the door to the bedroom, naked and deranged, and her daughter flew across the room and leaped into her arms. Olive fell to her knees, tears running hot down her face and onto Sylvie's shoulder.

"Mama," Sylvie said, "why are you crying?"

Because I was supposed to die in the pandemic but I was warned by a time traveller. Because a lot of people are going to die soon and there's nothing I can do to prevent it. Because nothing makes sense and I might be insane.

"I just missed you so much," Olive said.

"You missed me so much you had to come home early?" Sylvie asked.

"Yes," Olive said. "I missed you so much I had to come home early."

A strange alarm filled the room: Dion's device was blaring with a public alert. Over Sylvie's shoulder, Olive watched Dion staring at the screen. He looked up and saw her watching him.

"You were right," he said. "I'm sorry for doubting you. The virus is here."

For the first one hundred days of lockdown, Olive closed herself into her office every morning and sat at her desk, but it was easier to stare out the window than to write. Sometimes she just took notes on the soundscape.

Siren

Quiet; birds

Siren

Another siren

A third? Overlapping, from at least two directions

All quiet

Birds

Siren

The blur of passing days: Olive woke at four a.m. to work for two hours while Sylvie slept, then Dion worked from six a.m. to noon while Olive made an attempt to be a schoolteacher and to keep their daughter reasonably sane, then Olive worked for two hours while Dion and Sylvie played, then Sylvie got an hour of hologram time while both her parents worked, then Dion worked while Olive played with Sylvie, then somehow it was time to make dinner and then dinner blurred into the bedtime hour, then by eight p.m. Sylvie was asleep and Olive went to bed not long after, then Olive's alarm rang because it was once again four a.m., etc.

"We could think of it as an opportunity," Dion said, on the seventy-third night of lockdown. Olive and Dion were sitting together in the kitchen, eating ice cream. Sylvie was sleeping.

"An opportunity for what?" Olive asked. Even on Day 73, she still felt a little stunned. There was an element of incredulity— a pandemic? *Seriously?*—that hadn't quite faded.

"To think about how to re-enter the world," Dion said, "when re-entry is possible." There were certain friends he didn't miss, he said. He was quietly applying for new jobs.

"Let's pretend this seltzer bottle is a friend," Sylvie said, at dinner on Day 85. "Make it talk to me."

"Hello, Sylvie!" Olive said. She moved the glass bottle closer to Sylvie.

"Hi, bottle," Sylvie said.

In lockdown, there was a new kind of travel, but that didn't seem the right word. There was a new kind of anti-travel. In the evenings Olive keyed a series of codes into her device, donned a headset that covered her eyes, and entered the holospace. Holographic meetings had once been hailed as the way of the future—why go to the time and expense of physical travel, when one could transport oneself into a strange silvery-blank digital room and converse there with flickering simulations of one's colleagues?—but the unreality was painfully flat. Dion's job required a great many meetings, so he was in the holospace six hours a day and was dazed with exhaustion in the evenings.

"I don't know why it's so tiring," he said. "So much more tiring than normal meetings, I mean."

"I think it's because it isn't real." It was very late, and they were standing by the living room windows together, looking down at the deserted street.

"Maybe you're right. Turns out reality is more important than we thought," Dion said.

The thing with the tour—the thing with all the tours—is that there was no moment when she wasn't grateful, but also it was always too many faces. She'd always been shy. On tour all those faces kept appearing before her, face after face after face, and most of them were kind but all of them were the wrong faces, because after a few days on the road the only people Olive wanted to see were Sylvie and Dion.

But when the world shrank to the size of the interior of the apartment, and to a population of three, the people were what she missed. Where was the driver who was writing the book about the talking rats? She'd never even known the woman's name. Where was Aretta—the out-of-office message on Aretta's device was weeks out of date, which was worrying—and the other authors she'd met on that last tour, Ibby Mohammed and Jessica Marley? Where was the driver who sang an old jazz song as they drove through Tallinn, and the woman in Buenos Aires with the tattoo?

In lockdown, Colony Two was a strange, frozen place, silent except for the ambulance sirens and the soft *whir* of passing trolleys with their freight of masked medical workers. No one was supposed to go outside except for medical appointments and essential work, but on the one-hundredth night, while Sylvie was sleeping, Olive slipped out of the kitchen door and into the outside world. She moved swiftly and silently down the stairs to the garden, where she sat on the grass, under a small tree shaped like an umbrella. She was inches from the sidewalk but hidden by leaves. Being out of the apartment was disorienting. She was certain that the air here hadn't changed, but after her time on Earth it seemed wrong to her, flat and overly filtered. She stayed outdoors for an hour, then slipped back in with a sense of revelation. After that she went out every night to sit under the umbrella tree.

It was on one of those nights that the journalist appeared. The last journalist, as she'd always think of him, Gaspery-Jacques Roberts of *Contingencies Magazine*. On the night he appeared, she was under the umbrella tree, cross-legged on the grass, trying not to think of the day's numbers—752 dead today in Colony Two, with 3,458 new cases—and trying to let go of conscious thought, when she heard soft footsteps approaching. She didn't think it could be a patrol officer—they walked in pairs—but the fines for being outside in lockdown were steep, so she stayed very still and tried to breathe as quietly as possible.

The footsteps stopped, so close that she could see the person's shadow angled over the sidewalk. Could they have sensed her? It didn't seem possible. Someone else—another set of footsteps—was approaching, from the opposite direction.

"Zoey? What are you doing here?" Olive recognized the man's voice immediately, and her breath caught in her chest.

"I could ask you the same thing," a woman said. She had his accent.

"I told you in the travel chamber five minutes ago," Gaspery said. "I want to interview a literary scholar who interviewed Olive Llewellyn. One more layer of confirmation."

"I thought it was strange that you wanted to leave again after your interview with her, on an unscheduled trip," she said.

Gaspery didn't speak for a moment. "I thought you didn't travel anymore," he said finally.

"Yes, well, I felt the circumstances warranted an exception. Gaspery, how could you?"

"I was going to just talk to her," Gaspery said. "I was going to stick to the plan, but Zoey, I couldn't do it. I couldn't just let her die."

There was a moment of silence, during which both of these incomprehensible people were, Olive imagined, staring directly into her living room window. She looked up, but from her angle she could see only patches of the living room ceiling, mostly obscured by leaves.

"It's like you warned me," he said quietly. "You said the job required a lack of humanity, and it did. It does."

"You shouldn't come back to the present," Zoey said.

What?

"Of course I'll come back to the present," Gaspery said. "I believe in facing consequences."

"But the consequences will be terrible," Zoey said. "I've seen it happen before."

There was silence then. Gaspery didn't respond.

"The Night City's beautiful in this era," he said finally.

"I know." She was crying, Olive could hear it in her voice. "It isn't the Night City yet."

"You're right," he said. "The dome lighting still works. Are we standing on cobblestones?"

"Yes," she said, "I believe we are."

"There's a patrol coming," Gaspery said suddenly, and they were gone, walking quickly away together.

Olive stayed there for a long time in the shadows, in the strangeness. She was supposed to die in the pandemic, as she understood it, but then Gaspery had saved her. Hadn't he even told her what he was? *If a time traveller appeared before you . . .*

That night she looked up Gaspery-Jacques Roberts and the results were flooded with references to her own work, the book and the screen adaptation of *Marienbad*. She looked up *Contingencies Magazine,* and found a website with a few dozen articles, but the more she searched, the more it seemed like a front. It hadn't been updated in a long time, and its social media accounts were dormant.

She heard a small noise and started, but it was only Sylvie, standing in the doorway in unicorn pyjamas.

"Oh, sweetie," Olive said, "it's the middle of the night. Let me tuck you in."

"I have an insomnia," Sylvie said.

"I'll sit with you for a bit."

Olive lifted her daughter, this warm weight in her arms, and carried her back to her bedroom. Everything in the room was blue. Olive tucked her in under an indigo duvet and sat beside her. *I was supposed to die in the pandemic.*

"Could we play Enchanted Forest?" Sylvie asked.

"Of course," Olive said. "Let's play for a few minutes, till you feel sleepy." Sylvie shivered with delight. The Enchanted Forest was a new invention: Sylvie had never gone in for imaginary friends, but in lockdown she had an entire kingdom filled with them, and she was their queen.

"When I feel sleepy we'll stop," Sylvie said agreeably. "We'll stop before I fall asleep."

"The portal door opens," Olive said, because that was how the game always began. Sylvie's bedroom was quieter than Olive's office, being at the back of the building, but Olive still heard the faint wail of an ambulance siren.

"Who comes through?" Sylvie asked.

"Magic Foxy leaps through the portal. 'Queen Sylvie,' says Magic Foxy, 'come quickly! There's a problem in the Enchanted Forest!'"

Sylvie laughed, delighted. Magic Foxy was her favourite friend. "And only I can help, Magic Foxy?"

"'Yes, Queen Sylvie,' says Magic Foxy, 'only you can help.'"

Another lecture, this one virtual. No, the same lecture, just performed now in the holospace. (In non-space. Nowhere.) Olive was a hologram in a room of holograms, a sea of dim lights flickering before her, all of them gathered in a minimalistic suggestion of a room. She gazed out at several hundred slightly luminescent facsimiles of people, their actual bodies in individual rooms all over Earth and in the colonies, and had the unhinged thought that she was speaking directly to a congregation of souls.

"An interesting question," Olive said, "which I'd like to consider in these last few minutes, is why there's been such interest in postapocalyptic literature over this past decade or so. I've had the tremendous good fortune of getting to travel a great deal in the service of *Marienbad*—"

Blue sky over Salt Lake City, birds wheeling overhead
The rooftop of a hotel in Cape Town, lights sparkling in the trees
Wind rippling over a field of long grass by a train station in northern
England
"Can I show you my tattoo?" the woman in Buenos Aires said

"—which is to say I've had the opportunity to speak with a great many people about postapocalyptic literature. I've heard a great many theories about why there's such interest in the genre. One person suggested to me that it had to do with economic inequality, that in a world that can seem fundamentally unfair, perhaps we long to just blow everything up and start over—"

"That's just how it seems to me," the bookseller had said,
in an old shop in Vancouver, while Olive admired his pink glasses

"—and I'm not sure I agree with that, but it's an intriguing thought." The holograms shifted and stared. She liked the idea that she could still hold a room, even if now the room was just in the holospace, even if the room wasn't really a room. "Someone suggested to me that it has to do with a secret longing for heroism, which I found interesting. Perhaps we believe on some level that if the world were to end and be remade, if some unthinkable catastrophe were to occur, then perhaps we might be remade too, perhaps into better, more heroic, more honourable people."

"Doesn't it seem possible?" the librarian in Brazzaville asked,
her eyes shining, and outside on the street
someone was playing a trumpet,
"I mean, no one wants this to happen, obviously,
but think of the opportunity for heroism . . ."

"Some people have suggested to me that it's about the catastrophes on Earth, the decision to build domes over countless cities, the tragedy of being forced to abandon entire countries due to rising water or rising heat, but—"

A memory: waking in an airship between cities,
looking down at the dome over Dubai,
and believing for a wildly disorienting moment that she'd left Earth

"—that doesn't ring true to me. Our anxiety is warranted, and it's not unreasonable to suggest that we might channel that anxiety into fiction, but the problem with that theory is, our anxiety is nothing new. When have we ever believed that the world *wasn't* ending?

"I had a fascinating conversation with my mother once, where she talked about the guilt she and her friends had felt about bringing children into the universe. This was in the mid-2160s, in Colony Two. It's hard to imagine a more tranquil time or place, but they were concerned about asteroid storms, and if life on the moon became untenable, about the continued viability of life on Earth—"

> *Olive's mother drinking coffee in Olive's childhood home:*
> *yellow flowered tablecloth*
> *hands clasped around a blue coffee mug*
> *her smile*

"—and my point is, there's always something. I think, as a species, we have a desire to believe that we're living at the climax of the story. It's a kind of narcissism. We want to believe that we're uniquely important, that we're living at the end of history, that *now,* after all these millennia of false alarms, *now* is finally the worst that it's ever been, that finally we have reached the end of the world."

> *In a world that no longer exists but whose exact end date is unclear,*
> *Captain George Vancouver stands on the deck of the HMS Discovery,*
> *gazing anxiously out at a landscape with no people in it*

"But all of this raises an interesting question," Olive said. "What if it always *is* the end of the world?"

She paused for effect. Before her, the holographic audience was almost perfectly still. "Because we might reasonably think of the end of the world," Olive said, "as a continuous and never-ending process."

An hour later, Olive removed her headset and was once again alone in her office. She wasn't sure if she'd ever been so tired. She sat still for a while, absorbing the details of the physical world: the bookshelves, the framed drawings by Sylvie, the painting of a garden that her parents had given her as a wedding present, the odd piece of metal she'd once found on Earth that she'd hung on the wall because she loved the shape of it. She rose and went to the window to look out at the city. White street, white buildings, green trees, ambulance lights. It was midnight, and so the ambulances had no need of sirens. Lights flashed blue and red up the street and then receded.

I was supposed to die in the pandemic. She didn't entirely understand what that meant, and yet it was the point around which all of her thoughts revolved. A trolley passed, carrying medical workers, then another ambulance, then the stillness returned. Movement in the air: an owl flying silently through the dark.

"When we consider the question of why *now*," Olive said, before a different audience of holograms the following evening, "I mean why there's been this increased interest in postapocalyptic fiction over the past decade, I think we have to consider what's changed in the world in that timeframe, and that line of thinking leads me inevitably to our technology." A hologram in the front row was shimmering oddly, which meant the attendee had an unstable connection. "My personal belief is that we turn to postapocalyptic fiction not because we're drawn to disaster, per se, but because we're drawn to what we imagine might come next. We long secretly for a world with less technology in it."

"So I'm guessing I'm not the first to ask you what it's like to be the author of a pandemic novel during a pandemic," another journalist said.

"You might not be the very first."

Olive was standing by the window, staring up at the sky. The Colony Two dome had the same pixelations as Colonies One and Three, a shifting pattern of blue sky and clouds, but it seemed to her that there was a glitchy patch on the horizon, a section that flickered just slightly so that a square of black space showed through. It was hard to tell.

"What are you working on these days? Are you able to work?"

"I'm writing this crazy sci-fi thing," Olive said.

"Interesting. Can you tell me about it?"

"I don't know much about it myself, to be honest. I don't even know if it's a novel or a novella. It's actually kind of deranged."

"I suppose anything written this year is likely to be deranged," the journalist said, and Olive decided she liked her. "What drew you to sci-fi?"

That patch of sky had definitely just flickered. What would it look like if the dome lighting failed? It was a strange thought. She'd always taken the illusion of an atmosphere for granted.

"I've been in lockdown for one hundred and nine days," Olive said. "I think I just wanted to write something set as far away as possible from my apartment."

"Is that all it is?" the journalist asked. "Physical distance, a way of travelling during lockdown?"

"No, I guess not." An ambulance siren was approaching, and then the ambulance stopped in front of the building across the street. Olive turned her back to the window. "There's just . . . Look," Olive said, "I don't mean to be melodramatic, and I know it's like this in a lot of places now, but there's just, there is so much death. There's death all around us. I don't want to write about anything real."

The journalist was quiet.

"And I know it's like this for everyone else too. I know how fortunate I am. I know how much worse it could be. I'm not complaining. But my parents live on Earth, and I don't know if . . ." She had to stop and take a breath to compose herself. "I don't know when I'll see them again."

Two ambulances passed, one after the other, then silence. Olive looked over her shoulder. The ambulance across the street was still there.

"Are you there?" Olive asked.

"I'm sorry," the journalist said. Her voice was choked.

"What's your situation?" Olive asked softly. It occurred to her that the journalist sounded very young. She glanced at her calendar. The journalist's name was Annabel Escobar, and she worked in the city of Charlotte, which Olive dimly recalled visiting on a long-ago tour of United Carolina.

"I live alone," Annabel said. "We're not supposed to leave our houses, and it's just . . ." But she was crying now, truly weeping.

"I'm sorry," Olive said. "That sounds so lonely." She was staring out the window. The ambulance hadn't moved.

"I just haven't been in a room with anyone in a very long time," Annabel said.

On another night of searching, a centuries-old academic journal yielded a reference to a Gaspery J. Roberts. The journal had been devoted to prison reform. The hit sent Olive down a rabbit hole, at the end of which she found prison records from Earth: Gaspery J. Roberts had been sentenced to fifty years for a double homicide in Ohio in the late twentieth century. But there was no picture, so Olive couldn't be sure it was the same man.

"So, Olive," another journalist said. They were holograms in a silvery holospace room, along with two other authors who'd also written books whose plots involved pandemics. The four of them flickered like ghosts. "How many copies of *Marienbad* have you sold since the pandemic began?"

"Oh," Olive said. "I'm not sure. A lot."

"I know you've sold a lot," he said. "It's been on bestseller lists in a dozen Earth countries, all three moon colonies, and two of the three colonies on Titan. I'm asking you to be more specific."

"I'm afraid I don't have my sales numbers in front of me," Olive said. All of the holograms were staring at her.

"Really?" the journalist asked.

"It didn't occur to me to bring my royalty statements to this interview," Olive said.

An hour later, when the interview was over, she removed her headset and sat for a while with her eyes closed. She'd been home from Earth for long enough that when she opened the window, the night air of the Second Colony seemed fresh again. The air might be filtered, but there were plants, there was running water, there was a world outside her window as real as any world that anyone had ever lived in. Olive found herself thinking of Jessica Marley, for the first time in a while, and Jessica Marley's insufferable little coming-of-age-on-the-moon novel. Look, she wanted to tell her, there's no *pain in unreality* happening here. A life lived under a dome, in an artificially generated atmosphere, is still a life. A siren wailed and receded. Olive picked up her device, ran a search on Jessica's name, and discovered that she'd died two months ago in Spain.

"Mama?" Sylvie was in the doorway. "Is your interview over?"

"Hi, sweetie. Yes. It ended early." Jessica Marley was thirty-seven years old.

"Do you have another interview?"

"No." Olive knelt before her daughter, and then hugged her quickly. "No more till tomorrow."

"Then can we play Enchanted Forest?"

"Of course."

Sylvie wriggled a little in anticipation. *I was supposed to die in the pandemic.* Olive knew now that she was going to spend the rest of her life trying to understand that fact. But her effervescent five-year-old sat before her, grinning, and what she found at that moment, as the lights of yet another ambulance flickered over the ceiling, was that it was possible to smile back. This is the strange lesson of living in a pandemic: life can be tranquil in the face of death.

"Mama? Let's play Enchanted Forest."

"Okay," Olive said. "The portal door opens . . ."

6

Mirella and Vincent /

file corruption

1

Follow the evidence. In Gaspery's years of training, from the night he called Zoey to wish her a happy birthday through the present moment, that mantra had been a compass. *Present moment* was beginning to seem like a nonsensical term, but every moment can be distilled to a date, so let's call it November 30, 2203, in Colony Two, this city in the grip of a pandemic that would eventually kill 5 percent of its residents, this place that wasn't yet Gaspery's home and not yet the Night City, walking rapidly through the streets with Zoey to evade a lockdown-enforcement patrol.

"Here," Zoey said, and pulled him into a doorway. Gaspery peered through the glass door beside him, into a room of shadowy tables and chairs. This place was a restaurant, or had been. All of the restaurants in Colony Two were closed now.

They stood close together in the shadows, listening. All Gaspery could hear were sirens.

"You know you broke the most important protocol," Zoey said quietly. "Why did you do it?"

"I couldn't not warn her," Gaspery said.

"Okay," she said, "here's your situation. I've only done a preliminary analysis, but as far as I can tell, your decision to save Olive Llewellyn had no recognizable effect on the Time Institute."

"Does that mean I'll be okay?"

"No," she said, "it means you weren't immediately lost in time. It means your travel privileges haven't been revoked yet, because we sank five years of training into you and you still might be useful to the Time Institute, for at least the duration of this investigation. But if I were you, I'd get that tracker out of my arm and I wouldn't come back." She held up her device. "I have to go," she said. "Stay here, in this time, and I'll try to visit."

"Wait. Please."

She was still, watching him.

"I know you would never do what I did," he said. "But suppose you had done it. If you were in my position, Zoey, what would you do?"

"It's hard for me to imagine things that aren't real," she said.

"Can you try?"

Zoey sighed and closed her eyes. What occurred to Gaspery in that moment, watching her, was that he was her only person. Their parents were gone. She had never married. If she had friends or romantic interests, they'd never come up in conversation. He felt a fathomless guilt. Zoey opened her eyes.

"I might try to solve the anomaly," she said.

"How?"

Zoey was quiet for so long that he thought she wasn't going to answer. "Hold on," she said. "It took our best research teams a year to figure out these coordinates." She typed something into her device, and he heard his own device chime softly in his pocket.

"I sent you a new destination," Zoey said. "We don't know the time, we only know the day and the place, so you'll have to wait in the forest." She entered another code into her device and blinked out.

Gaspery was alone in the doorway, in the right city but the wrong time. He closed his eyes and considered the course of the investigation, because that was preferable to thinking about his sister, or thinking of what awaited him if he returned to his own time. He had a new destination. He entered the codes into his device, and he left.

2

He was on the beach at Caiette. He could see from the coordinates that he'd landed in the summer of 1994, but at first it seemed like a mistake, because the place hadn't changed at all over the past eight decades. He was staring at two little islands, tufts of trees across the water, and for a disorienting moment he thought he was back in 1912, dressed in the costume of an early-twentieth-century priest, preparing to meet Edwin St. Andrew in the church.

The little white church on the hillside was unchanged since the last time he'd been here—it must have recently been repainted—but the houses around it were different. He turned his back on the settlement, and his gaze fell on the ocean. The sun was rising, shades of blue and pink rippling over the water. He liked the way it moved, the gentle repetition of waves. He found himself thinking of his mother now, for the first time in a while. She'd spent time on Earth as a child. She'd kept a framed photo of an Earth ocean in the kitchen of his childhood home, a small rectangle of waves on the wall near the stove. He remembered her gazing at it while she stirred soup. And yet for himself, he realized, the ocean carried no weight in his heart, it featured in none of his childhood memories and none of the important moments of his life; it was just a place he'd seen in movies and visited for work, so he couldn't summon much feeling for it, and after a moment he turned and walked away down the beach, following the coordinates that flashed softly on his device. He walked beyond the last house, then into the forest.

Walking through this forest was easier now than when he'd been wearing a priest's robe, but he still had no talent for it. The ground was too soft; branches caught at his clothes; he felt assailed from all sides. It was a sunny afternoon, but it must have rained that morning. Ferns pulled wetly at his legs. His shoes were less waterproof than he'd thought. His device pulsed softly in his hand, with a message that he was very close to the place he sought; he let go of the branch he'd been holding to study the screen, and the branch slapped him across the face.

Here was the maple tree, eighty-two years older than the last time he'd seen it. It had gained less in height than in breadth and magnificence. The clearing around it had widened with the passage of time. He walked under the canopy of its branches, to look up at the sunlight shifting through leaves, and for the first time in memory, he felt true reverence.

When would Vincent Smith come here? There was no way to

know. Gaspery stepped just outside the clearing, and fought his way into a thicket of dense leaves, where he knelt on the cool, wet earth, and waited.

He was very still, listening. Another thing he didn't like about forests was the constant sound. It wasn't the steady white noise of the moon cities, the distant mechanicals that increased the gravity to Earth levels and kept the air inside the domes breathable and created the illusion of a breeze. There was no pattern to the white noise of a forest, and the randomness put Gaspery on edge. Time passed, hours. His muscles cramped. He was desperately thirsty. He stood a few times, to stretch, then crouched low again. It was impossible to hear anything coming, until it wasn't. A little after four in the afternoon, he heard the girl's soft footsteps on the path.

Vincent Smith at thirteen: she looked like she'd cut her own hair with blunt scissors before she'd dyed it bright blue. Her eyes were ringed in black. She radiated neglect. She walked slowly, looking through the viewfinder of her camera, and from his hiding place Gaspery recognized the scene: once he'd sat in a theatre in New York City and watched a somewhat tedious musical performance accompanied by the footage that Vincent was creating at this moment. She stopped under the tree, angled the camera upward—

—*and reality broke: Gaspery and Vincent were in the cavernous echoing cathedral of the Oklahoma City Airship Terminal, where Olive Llewellyn was walking just ahead of them and notes were rising from a nearby violin. And here too, impossibly, was Edwin St. Andrew, face upturned toward the branches/the terminal ceiling—*

Vincent staggered and all but dropped her camera. Gaspery's hands were clasped over his mouth, because he wanted to scream, and the terminal was gone. It's one thing to know in the abstract that one moment might corrupt another moment; it's another to experience both moments at once; it's something else again to suspect what it might mean. Vincent was staring around wildly, but Gaspery was crouched low and she didn't see him. He closed his eyes, sank his hands into the mud, and tried to convince himself that the cold water seeping through the knees of his pants was real.

3

But what makes a world real?

Gaspery was lying on his back in the mud, staring up at leaves silhouetted against a darkening sky, and it seemed to him that he'd been there for some time. Night was falling in the forest. Vincent was gone. He sat up, with some effort—his back was stiff; how long had he been lying there unmoving?—and sent a message through his device: *I saw it! I saw the file corruption! It's real, Zoey.*

There was no reply. He knew what he'd done, he knew he'd broken the most important rule by saving Olive Llewellyn, but he retained a sliver of hope that the message might save him.

4

Gaspery returned to the moment he'd left, to Travel Room Eight in the third sub-basement of the Time Institute, Zoey sitting before him at the control desk.

"I saw it," Gaspery said. "I saw the anomaly."

"I got your message." Zoey was staring at him, and he saw that she'd been crying. "I just spoke with Ephrem," she said. "You're being taken out of commission."

"What will happen to me?"

"Nothing good."

"I know what I did," Gaspery said. "But if I finish the investigation, maybe they'll . . ."

"I don't think there's anything you can do to save yourself now."

"But there *might* be. Look. I just want another level of confirmation, another witness. I need two more destinations." Gaspery stepped out of the machine, and handed over his device.

She looked at it and frowned. "1918?"

"I have follow-up questions for Edwin St. Andrew."

"In 1918? He experienced the anomaly in 1912. And what's in 2007?"

"A party Vincent Smith attended," he said. "Or I guess she's Vincent Alkaitis by that point. The party was on a list of secondary destinations."

"But your device and your tracker are out of commission," she said.

"Zoey," Gaspery said. "Please."

She closed her eyes for just a moment, and then took his device. She was typing something that he couldn't see, then she leaned close to the projection for an iris scan. "I'm overriding the decommissioning order," she said. Her voice was strangely flat, and he saw terror in her eyes. "Ephrem will be here any minute, probably with security forces. I won't stop you from going, Gaspery, but I can't protect you if you come back."

"I understand," he said. "Thank you."

Gaspery heard the knock on the door just as he was leaving.

5

Gaspery stepped out of a New York City men's room in the winter of 2007, into the warmth and light of a party in an art gallery. He moved slowly through the crowd, trying to orient himself. He was looking for Vincent Smith. He knew she'd be here—her presence had been entered into the historical record, because somewhere in this room was a society photographer—but what that meant, in 2007, was that Mirella Kessler was here too, and after his strange encounter with her in 2020, Gaspery hoped to avoid her.

He saw them together at the far end of the room, admiring a large-scale oil painting. He plucked a glass of red wine from a little round tray and went to stare at a different painting and plot his next move. He was utterly unnerved by the crowd. They were shaking hands, which even after all of his cultural-sensitivity training seemed like a bizarre thing to do in flu season, and kissing one another on the cheek. These people have no direct experience of pandemics, he reminded himself. None of them were old enough to remember the winter of 1918–1919; Ebola was a few years out and would mostly be confined to the other side of the Atlantic; Covid-19 would not arrive for another thirteen years. Gaspery began moving slowly around the periphery of the room, sidling toward Vincent.

In 2007, Vincent was wealthy, and possessed of a sheen of elegance and self-confidence that he wouldn't have expected of the blue-haired waif he'd just encountered in Caiette. Her arm was looped through Mirella's, and they were standing in front of a painting, but, he saw now, not really looking at it. They were speaking in a conspiratorial way. Mirella laughed softly. They had a look of inseparability that brought him close to despair. But then Vincent extricated herself to say hello to someone else, while Mirella turned to find her husband, and Gaspery saw his chance.

"Vincent?"

"Hello." She had a warm smile, and he found that he liked her immediately.

"I'm sorry to bother you. I'm conducting an investigation on behalf of an art collector, and I wondered if I might ask you a quick question about your brother Paul's videos."

He had her attention. Her eyes widened. "My brother? But I didn't think—I didn't know he did videos. He's a musician. Or a composer, I guess."

"That's my suspicion," he said. "I don't think he shot those videos. I think someone else did."

She frowned. "Can you describe them?"

"Well, there's one in particular," Gaspery said. "The videographer was walking through a forest. British Columbia, I think. It was a sunny day. Judging by the quality of the footage, I'd say probably sometime in the mid-nineties."

Her gaze softened. Gaspery had a sense of performing some kind of hypnosis. "The videographer walked along a path," he continued, "toward a maple tree."

She nodded. "I used to record on that path all the time," she said.

"On this particular video, something strange happens. There's this weird flash of something," Gaspery said, "like it all goes dark for a second, probably just some kind of glitch on the tape—"

"It seemed like a glitch," Vincent said, "but it wasn't on the tape."

"You saw it?"

"I heard these weird noises, and everything went dark."

"What did you hear?"

"Violin music. Then a noise like hydraulics. It was inexplicable." Her eyes focused suddenly. "I'm sorry," she said, "what did you say your name was?"

Her husband was moving through the crowd toward them, he was handing Vincent a glass of wine, and Gaspery took advantage of this momentary distraction to slip away from them. He felt a strange elation that was equal parts exhaustion and joy. He had a corroborating interview, recorded on his device. He had his own observations. For the first time since his interview with Olive Llewellyn, on the morning of this strange and seemingly infinite day, he felt he might not be doomed.

But Gaspery hesitated by the men's room door for a moment, watching the party, and his happiness faded. Here was the awfulness that Zoey had warned him of, the utterly miserable knowledge of how everyone else's stories would end. He looked out over the room, and for the first time in his life, Gaspery felt old.

Vincent and her husband clinked their glasses together. In fourteen months Alkaitis would be arrested for running a massive Ponzi scheme, then released on bail, at which point he would flee to Dubai—abandoning Vincent—and live out the rest of his long life in a series of hotels.

Vincent would live for another twelve years, and then disappear under mysterious circumstances from the deck of a container ship.

Nearby was Mirella, talking with her husband, Faisal. Faisal was an investor in Jonathan's fraud scheme, and when the scheme collapsed in a year he would lose everything, as would the family members who'd invested at his urging. Faisal would die of suicide.

Mirella would find the body, and the note. Then she would remain for more than a decade in New York City, until in March 2020 she would travel to Dubai for unknown reasons, arriving just in time to be stranded by the Covid-19 pandemic.

There she would meet Himesh Chiang, a guest at the same hotel where she was staying, and after some time the two of them would return to his native London, where they would survive the pandemic, marry, and live out the rest of their lives together; she would give birth to three children, have a successful career in retail management, and die of pneumonia at eighty-five, a year after her husband's death in a car accident.

But so much is inevitably left out of any biography, any accounting of any life. Before all of that, before Mirella lost Faisal, before this party in this city by the sea, she'd been a child in Ohio. Gaspery shivered. He was thinking of the way she'd looked at him in the park, in January 2020. *You were under the overpass,* she'd said to him, with terrible certainty, *in Ohio, when I was a kid.* Not just that. She'd said he was arrested there.

He'd been thinking of 1918 as his final trip. He had made every effort to save himself, and after 1918 he was going home to face the consequences. But what he realized now, watching Mirella, was that it was too late. He was going to go to 1918, but there would be one more destination after that.

Remittance /

1918, 1990, 2008

1

In 1918 Edwin had no more brothers, and only one foot. He lived with his parents on the family estate. He walked constantly, ostensibly because he was trying to improve his gait—he'd been fitted with a prosthetic and walked in a lurching way—but really because if he stopped moving, the enemy might get him. He walked at all hours of the day and night. Sleep transported him reliably back to the trenches, so he avoided sleep, which meant it ambushed him unexpectedly: while reading in the library, while sitting in the garden, once or twice at dinner.

His parents weren't sure how to speak to him, or how to look at him even. They couldn't accuse him of shiftlessness anymore, because he was a war hero but also something of an invalid. It was obvious to everyone that he wasn't well. "You've changed so much, darling," his mother said gently, and he wasn't sure whether this was a compliment, an accusation, or pure observation. He'd never been good at reading people and now he was worse.

"Well," he said, "I saw some things I wish I hadn't."

Understatement of the goddamned twentieth century.

He felt more empathy for his mother than previously, though. When Abigail floated off at the dinner table, when talk turned to the colonies and the look that her sons had once unkindly termed her British India expression came over her face, Edwin understood more vividly now that she was mourning a loss. He still found the Raj indefensible, but that didn't mean she hadn't lost an entire world. It wasn't her fault that the world she'd grown up in had ceased to exist.

Sometimes in the garden, he liked to talk to Gilbert, although Gilbert was dead. Gilbert and Niall had both died in the Battle of the Somme, a day apart, while Edwin had survived Passchendaele. No, *survived* was the wrong word. Edwin's animate body had returned from Passchendaele. He thought of his body now in strictly mechanical terms. His heart flapped deathlessly. He continued to breathe. He was in good physical health, except for the missing foot, but he was fundamentally unsound. It was difficult to be alive in the world.

"It's not uncommon," he heard the doctor say in the corridor outside his room, in the earliest weeks, when all he did was lie in bed. "The boys who went over there and wound up in the trenches, well, some of them saw things none of us should."

He hadn't entirely surrendered. He was making an effort. He rose and dressed in the mornings now, he ate the food that appeared in front of him at the table, and then, his strength exhausted, he spent most of the remaining day in the garden. He liked to sit out there on a bench under a tree and talk to Gilbert. He knew Gilbert wasn't there—he wasn't *that* far gone—but there was no one else to talk to. He'd had friends here, once, but now one friend was in China and all the others were dead.

"Now that you and Niall are dead," he confided, to Gilbert, "I'll inherit the title and the estate." He was surprised by how little he cared.

It came as an odd jolt when he walked out into the walled garden one morning and saw a man waiting on the bench. For just a heartbeat he thought it was Gilbert—at this point anything seemed possible—but then he came closer and the man's true identity was almost as strange: he was the impostor from that tiny church on the westernmost edge of British Columbia, the strange man in the clothes of a priest whom no one else in that place had ever seen or heard of.

"Please," the man said. "Sit." That same unplaceable foreign accent.

Edwin sat beside him on the bench.

"I thought you were a hallucination," Edwin said. "When I

saw Father Pike and asked him about the new priest I'd just been speaking to, Pike looked at me like I had two heads."

"My name is Gaspery-Jacques Roberts," the stranger said. "I'm afraid I only have a few minutes, but I wanted to see you."

"A few minutes until what?"

"An appointment. You'll think I'm a lunatic if I tell you the details."

"I'm afraid I'm in no position to judge anyone else's lunacy, just at present, but why are you lurking around my garden?"

Gaspery hesitated. "You were on the Western Front, weren't you?"

Mud. Cold rain. An explosion, blinding light, things raining down around him, then one of those things hit him in the chest and when he looked down he recognized his best friend's arm—

"Belgium," Edwin confirmed, through gritted teeth.

Friend wasn't really the word for what that man was to him, actually. The thing that hit his jacket and fell to his feet was the arm of his beloved. His beloved's head landed nearby in the mud, eyes still wide with amazement.

"And now you fear for your sanity," Gaspery said carefully.

"It was always a little fragile, in all honesty," Edwin said.

"Do you remember what you saw in the forest at Caiette? It was years ago now."

"Vividly, but it was a hallucination. The first of many, I'm afraid."

Gaspery was quiet for a moment. "I can't explain the mechanics here," he said. "My sister probably could, but it's still beyond me. But whatever happened to you afterward, whatever you saw in Belgium, it's possible you're saner than you think. I can assure you that what you saw in Caiette was real."

"How do I know that you're real?" Edwin asked.

Gaspery reached out his hand, and touched Edwin's shoulder. They stayed like that for a moment, Edwin staring at the hand on his shoulder, then Gaspery removed his hand and Edwin cleared his throat.

"What I experienced in Caiette couldn't possibly have been real," Edwin said. "It was a derangement of the senses."

"Was it? I believe you heard a few notes of violin music, played by a musician in an airship terminal in the year 2195."

"An airship . . . the year twenty-one-*what*?"

"Followed by a sound that must have seemed quite strange to you. A sort of *whoosh*, wasn't it?"

Edwin stared at him. "How did you know?"

"Because that's the sound that airships make," Gaspery said. "They won't be invented for some time. As for the violin music . . . a kind of lullaby, wasn't it?" He was quiet for a beat, then hummed a few notes. Edwin gripped the armrest of the bench. "The man who composed that song won't be born for another hundred and eighty-nine years."

"None of this is possible," Edwin said.

Gaspery sighed. "Think of it in terms of . . . well, in terms of corruption. Moments in time can corrupt one another. There was a derangement, but it had nothing to do with you. You're just a man who saw it. You were helpful in my investigation, and

I believe you're in a somewhat delicate state, and I thought perhaps it might ease your mind just a little to know that you might be saner than you think. At that moment, at least, you were not hallucinating. You were experiencing a moment from elsewhere in time."

Edwin's gaze drifted away from the man's face, to the mild decrepitude of the September garden. The salvias were bare now, for the most part, brown stalks and dried leaves, a few last blooms wisping blue and violet in the failing light. He was struck by an understanding of what his life could be from this moment: he could live here quietly, and care for the garden, and that might eventually be enough.

"Thank you for telling me," Edwin said.

"Don't tell anyone else." Gaspery rose, brushing a fallen leaf from his jacket. "You'll get committed to an asylum."

"Where are you going?" Edwin asked.

"I've an appointment in Ohio," Gaspery said. "Good luck."

"Ohio?"

But Gaspery was already walking away from him, disappearing around the side of the house. Edwin watched him go and then remained on his bench for a long time, hours, watching the way the garden faded into twilight.

2

Gaspery walked around the side of the house, and in the shadows at the base of a weeping willow, he stood staring at his device
for a moment. A message pulsed softly on the screen: *Return*.
He had exhausted the limits of his itinerary. The only possible
destination was home. For just a moment he entertained a wild
notion of staying here in 1918, burying his device in the garden
and cutting his tracker out of his arm, taking his chances in the
flu pandemic and trying to find some kind of life for himself in a
foreign world, but even as he thought this he was already entering the code, he was already leaving, and when he opened his
eyes in the harsh light of the Time Institute, he was unsurprised
to see the figures gathered there, the men and women in black
uniforms waiting with weapons drawn. What was surprising,
though, was that Olive Llewellyn's publicist was standing next to
Ephrem. They were the only two out of uniform.

"Aretta?"

"Hello, Gaspery," she said.

"Stay where you are, please," Ephrem said. "There's no need to leave the machine." His hands were clasped behind his back. Gaspery stayed where he was. At the back of the room—he had to crane his neck to see around the black uniforms—Zoey was being restrained by two men.

"I never guessed," Gaspery said, to Aretta.

"That's because I'm competent at my job," Aretta said. "I don't go around telling people I'm a time traveller."

"That's fair." Gaspery felt a little unhinged. "I'm sorry," he said to Zoey. "I'm sorry I tricked you." But she was already being escorted from the room, the door closing behind her.

"You tricked her?" Ephrem asked.

"I told her I was going to 1918 as part of the investigation. I was really there to try to save Edwin St. Andrew from dying in an insane asylum."

"Seriously, Gaspery? Yet another crime? Does someone have an updated bio?"

Aretta was frowning at her device. "Updated bio," she said. "Thirty-five days after Gaspery's visit, Edwin St. Andrew died in the 1918 flu pandemic."

"Isn't that the same bio?" Ephrem reached for her device, read for a moment, then handed it back with a sigh. "If you hadn't changed the time line," he said to Gaspery, "he still would've died of the flu, just forty-eight hours later and in an insane asylum. You see how *pointless* that was?"

"You're missing the point," Gaspery said.

"That's very possible." Were there tears in Ephrem's eyes? He looked tired and strained. A man who'd preferred being an arborist; a man in a difficult position, doing a difficult job. "Is there anything you'd like to say?"

"Are we at last words already, Ephrem?"

"Well, last words in this century," Ephrem said. "Last words on the moon. I'm afraid you'll be travelling some distance and not returning."

"Can you take care of my cat?" Gaspery asked.

Ephrem blinked.

"Yes, Gaspery, I'll take care of your cat."

"Thank you."

"Is there anything else?"

"I'd do it again," Gaspery said. "I wouldn't even hesitate."

Ephrem sighed. "Good to know." He'd been holding a glass bottle behind his back. He raised it now, and misted something in Gaspery's face. There was a sweet scent, a dimming of the lights, then Gaspery's legs were giving way—

3

—as he faded out, he had an impression that Ephrem had stepped into the machine behind him—

4

—Two gunshots, in quick succession—

Footsteps, a man running away—

Gaspery was in a tunnel. Light at either end, not just light but snow—

No, not a tunnel, an overpass. He could smell the exhaust of twentieth-century cars. He was very sleepy, from whatever he'd just been misted with. His back was to the embankment.

Ephrem was there too, calm and efficient in his dark suit. "I'm sorry, Gaspery," he said softly, his breath warm in Gaspery's ear. "I really am." He plucked Gaspery's device from his hand and replaced it with something hard and cold and much heavier—

A gun. Gaspery looked at it, curious, and the running man—the shooter, he realized dimly—disappeared, scrambling away and out of sight. Ephrem was gone too, a passing ghost. The air was cold.

He heard a soft groan near his feet. It was difficult for Gaspery to stay awake. His eyes kept closing. But he saw two men lying nearby, two men whose blood was seeping across the concrete, and one of them was staring directly at him. There was clear confusion in the man's stare—*Who are you? Where did you come from?*—but he'd passed beyond speaking, and as Gaspery watched, the light left his eyes. Gaspery was alone under an expressway with two dead men. He nodded off, just for a moment. When he opened his eyes, he was staring at the gun in his hand, and the pieces of the puzzle were drifting together. *It's possible to get lost in time,* Zoey had said, in a different century. Why go to the bother of incarcerating a man for life on the moon, when that man can be sent elsewhere, framed, and imprisoned at someone else's expense?

He sensed movement to his left. He turned his head, very slowly, and saw the children. Two girls, aged perhaps nine and eleven, holding hands. They'd been walking under the overpass, but now they'd stopped some distance away, staring. He saw their backpacks, and realized they were on their way home from school.

Gaspery let the gun fall from his hand, and it clattered away like a harmless thing. There were lights washing over him now, red and blue. The girls were staring at the two dead men, then the younger girl looked at him, and he recognized her.

"Mirella," he said.

5

No star burns forever. Gaspery scratched the words on a wall in prison some years later, so delicately that from any distance at all it looked like a flaw in the paint. You had to get close to see it, and you had to have lived in the twenty-second century or later to know what it meant. You had to have seen that twenty-second-century press conference, the president of China on a podium with a half-dozen of her favourite world leaders arrayed behind her, flags snapping against a brilliant blue sky.

There was time in prison, infinite time, so Gaspery spent a lot of it thinking about the past, no, the future, the point in time in which he'd walked into Zoey's office on her birthday with cupcakes and flowers, and everything that had followed. What had happened now was terrible, he was in prison in the wrong century and he was going to die here, but as months slipped into years, he found his regrets were very few. Warning Olive Llewellyn of the approaching pandemic was not, no matter how he turned the moment over in his mind, the wrong thing to do. If someone's about to drown, you have a duty to pull them from the water. His conscience was clear.

"What's that you wrote there, Roberts?" Hazelton asked. Hazelton was his cellmate, a much younger man who paced and talked incessantly. Gaspery didn't mind him.

"No star burns forever," Gaspery said.

Hazelton nodded. "I like that," he said. "Power of positive thinking, right? You're in prison, but that's not forever, because nothing is *forever,* right? Me, every time I start feeling a little down about my life, I—" He kept talking, but Gaspery stopped listening. He was calm these days, in a way he wouldn't have expected. In the early evenings Gaspery liked to sit on the farthest possible edge of his bunk, almost falling off the end, because from that angle there was a sliver of sky visible through the window, and through it he could see the moon.

8

Anomaly

1

Is this the promised end?

A line from Olive Llewellyn's novel *Marienbad,* but really a
quote from Shakespeare. I found it in the prison library five or
six years in, in a paperback with a missing cover.

2

No star burns forever.

3

Not long after my sixtieth birthday I developed some heart trouble, the kind of thing that could have been easily fixed in my own century but was dangerous in this time and place, and I was transferred to the prison hospital. I couldn't see the moon from my bed, so there was nothing for it now but to close my eyes and play old movies:

walking to school in the Night City, past Olive Llewellyn's childhood home
with its boarded-up front window and plaque;
standing in the church in Caiette in 1912 in my priest costume,
waiting for Edwin St. Andrew to stagger in;
chasing squirrels when I was five in the strip of wilderness
between the Night City dome and the Periphery Road;
drinking with Ephrem behind the school on an afternoon without

sunlight when we were fifteen or so, one of those afternoons that felt a
little dangerous,
even though all we were doing was getting slightly drunk and
trading dumb jokes;
holding hands and laughing with my mother on a
sunlit day in the Night City when I was six or seven,
stopping to look down at the river from a
pedestrian bridge, the river dark and sparkling below—

"Gaspery."

I felt a sharp pain in my arm. I gasped and almost cried out, but a hand was over my mouth.

"Shh," Zoey whispered. She looked like she was in her early forties, she was wearing a nurse's uniform, and she had just cut the tracker out of my arm. I stared at her, uncomprehending.

"I'm going to place this under your tongue," she said. She held it up for me to see: a new tracker, to correspond with the new device that she was pressing into my hand. She had drawn the curtain around my bed. She held her device against mine for a second or two, until the devices flashed in a quick coordinated pattern. I stared at those lights—

4

—and we were in a different room, in a different place.

I was lying on my back on a wood floor, in a bedroom, in what seemed to me to be an old-fashioned kind of house. My arm was bleeding; I held it reflexively to my chest. Sunlight poured in through a window. I sat up. There was wallpaper with roses, wooden furniture, and through a doorway I saw a room with a shower and a toilet.

"What is this place?"

"This is a farm on the outskirts of Oklahoma City," she said. "I've paid a great deal of money to the owners, and you can stay here indefinitely, as a boarder. The year is 2172."

"2172," I said. "So in twenty-three years, I'll visit Oklahoma City to interview the violinist."

"Yes."

"How are you here? Surely the Time Institute didn't approve this trip."

"I was arrested that day," she said. "The day you were sent to Ohio. I had tenure and an otherwise sterling record, so I wasn't lost in time, but I spent a year in prison and then immigrated to the Far Colonies. The Time Institute thinks they have the only functional time machine in existence. They don't."

"There's a time machine in the Far Colonies? And you just, what, get to use it?"

"I'm employed by . . . another organization there," she said.

"Even with your record?"

"Gaspery," she said, "no one's better than me at what I do." She spoke matter-of-factly; she wasn't boasting.

"You know, I still don't know what that is."

She ignored this. "I made this mission a condition of my agreeing to take the job in the Far Colonies," she said. "I'm sorry I couldn't come sooner. I mean to an earlier point in time."

"It's okay. I mean, thank you. Thank you for coming for me."

"I think it's safe here, Gaspery. I built a paper trail for you. You should settle in. Meet the neighbours."

"Zoey, I can't thank you enough."

"You'd do the same for me." (Unspoken between us: I *couldn't* do the same for her. She was of a different order from me, and always had been.) "I don't know if we'll see each other again," Zoey said.

Had we ever hugged before? I couldn't remember. She clasped me close for just a moment, stepped back, and was gone.

I was alone in the room, but *alone* wasn't a strong enough word for it. I knew no one in this century, and the fact of having been through this before did nothing to assuage my loneliness. I had a deranged moment of wondering how Hazelton was doing, then remembered that my cellmate would have died of old age by now.

I went to the window, in a daze, and looked out at a sea of green. The farm reached almost to the horizon, field upon field with agricultural robots moving slowly in the sunlight. In the far distance, I saw the spires of Oklahoma City. The sky was a dazzling blue.

5

The farm was owned and run by an older couple, Clara and Mariam. They were in their late eighties and had been here all their lives. They were pleased to have a well-paying boarder, they told me that first night, over a dinner of quiche and the freshest salad I'd tasted in decades, and they would ask me no questions. They respected privacy above all.

"Thank you," I said.

"Your sister left us some identity paperwork for you," Clara said. "Birth certificate and such. Shall we call you by the name on the paperwork?"

"Call me Gaspery," I said. "Please."

"Well, Gaspery," Clara said, "should you ever have need of your documents, it's all in that blue cabinet by the hallway door."

I didn't leave the farm at all those first few years, but I feared that eventually I'd have to. When Mariam fell ill, Clara drove her to the hospital, but who would drive Clara? They were nearing ninety. *My first case at the Institute involved a doppelgänger,* Ephrem had told me once, in another, unfathomable life. *According to our best facial-recognition software, the same woman appeared in photographs and video footage taken in 1925 and 2093.* Whenever I imagined leaving the farm, I imagined surveillance cameras picking up my face and setting off alarms through the centuries, a Time Institute agent arriving to investigate, a cascade of horrors. I spoke with Clara, who made discreet inquiries with a neighbour, who had a friend with useful contacts, and a short time later I was lying on my back on the farmhouse kitchen table, undergoing laser facial resculpting and iris recolouring.

When the sedation wore off and I sat up, the surgeon was gone.

"Whisky?" Mariam asked.

"Please," I said.

"You look completely different," Clara said. She passed me a mirror, and I gasped.

I did look completely different. But I recognized my face.

6

Later that month, I found the violin. It was very old, and in a box at the very back of the hall closet; Mariam hadn't played it in years. Clara arranged for lessons from a neighbour.

"She goes by Lina," Clara said on the drive over. "She's been playing violin all her life, in my understanding. Came here in much the same manner as you, if you get my drift."

I glanced at her. She was ninety-two that year, but her profile was still strong. Her eyes were unreadable.

"I had no idea," I said. There must have been a note of reproach in this, because Clara fixed me for a beat or two in her calm gaze.

"You know I believe in privacy," she said. "So does she, by all appearances. She's barely left that farm in thirty years."

We pulled up at the neighbouring farmhouse—a grey cubist monstrosity that could have served as a hotel—and I was thinking of Zoey's words when she left me here, four years ago now—*You should settle in. Meet the neighbours*—and wondering why I'd never been able to properly apprehend anything she'd ever said. I stepped out of the truck into glaring sunlight.

The front door opened, and the woman who stepped out was around my age, early sixties.

"Good morning, Gaspery," Talia said.

7

"Your sister probably got me out just in time," Talia told me. "She came to the hotel one night, must have been right after she got out of prison, and told me the police had opened a file on me, something about repeating classified information."

"Well, in fairness, you did have a habit of repeating classified information." We were sitting on the porch of the farmhouse where she lived, our violins resting between us.

"I was reckless. Tempting fate, I suppose. She said she was about to move to the Far Colonies, and strongly suggested I come with her, but the Far Colonies have an extradition treaty with the moon, so she suggested once we got there that perhaps that shouldn't be my final destination."

"And that was thirty years ago?"

"Twenty-six."

I could see it when I looked at her, that quarter-century of living on this farm. Her skin was darkened by the sun and she had
a peacefulness about her.

"What are they like?" I asked. "The Far Colonies?"

"They're beautiful," she said, "but I didn't like living underground."

8

We were married within a year, Talia and I, and when Clara and Mariam died, they left the farm to us.

This, I found myself thinking in the years that followed, on nights when my wife and I played the violin together, when we cooked together, when we walked in our fields watching the movements of the farm robots, when we sat on the porch watching the airships rise up like fireflies on the horizon over Oklahoma City, this is what the Time Institute never understood: if definitive proof emerges that we're living in a simulation, the correct response to that news will be *So what*. A life lived in a simulation is still a life.

9

A countdown had begun. I sensed it in the background of all my days. Sometime soon, I knew, I would move to Oklahoma City. I was scheduled to begin playing the violin in the airship terminal by 2195. I knew, because I remembered the interview, that my wife was going to die first.

10

Quietly
in the night
of an aneurysm
when she was seventy-five.

11

When Talia was gone I sat alone on the porch every night for a while, watching the airships rising over the distant city. My dog, Odie, lay beside me, head on his paws. At first I thought I was putting off moving to the city because I loved the farm, but one night it hit me: I *longed* for those lights. After all this time, I wanted to be around people again.

"I'll take you with me," I told Odie, who wagged his tail.

12

What someone—anyone!—at the Time Institute really should have caught, given how intelligent everyone was supposed to be over there, was that I was the anomaly. No, that's not fair. I *triggered* the anomaly. How did no one catch that I was interviewing myself? Because thanks to the documentation Zoey had created, on paper my name was Alan Sami and I'd been born and spent my life on a farm outside of Oklahoma City.

I watched the anomaly from the airship terminal. On an October day in 2195, I was playing the violin, my dog beside me, and I noticed two people almost at the same time.

Olive Llewellyn was walking along the corridor, pulling her silver suitcase. She didn't notice the man walking toward me a few metres ahead of her, but I did. The man had just stepped out of a utility closet.

As the man walked toward me, crossing Olive Llewellyn's path, the air seemed to ripple behind him. He didn't notice, because he was focused on me, and because he was a little anxious; this was, after all, his first interview for the Time Institute.

I kept playing, sweating now, holding on for dear life to my lullaby for Talia. The rippling intensified; the software, if that was the word for it, whatever unknowable engine kept our world intact, was struggling to reconcile the impossibility of both of us being here. But it wasn't just that the same person was in the same place twice; the engine, the intelligence, the software, whatever it was, it had detected a third Gaspery, somewhere else altogether in time and space, in the forest at Caiette, and now things were truly coming apart: this moment was corrupted, but so was *that place,* that point in the forest where in 1912 Edwin St. Andrew gazed up into the branches, where in 1994 I hid behind ferns and watched Vincent Smith. There was a strange wave of darkness behind the approaching man, light rippling away. Olive Llewellyn stopped as if struck. I saw myself kneeling in 1994, and Edwin St. Andrew in exactly the same spot—we were superimposed on one another—and nearby was Vincent Smith, thirteen years old with a camera in her hand.

An airship ascended at a nearby port, that unmistakable *whoosh,* and the spectres were gone. Time was running smoothly again. The file corruption was repairing itself, the threads of the simulation knitting into place around us, and Gaspery-Jacques Roberts, my younger self, new recruit and distressingly inept investigator for the Time Institute, had noticed none of it. It had all transpired behind his back. He did glance over his shoulder, but—I remembered the moment—chalked up his overwhelming sense of wrongness to runaway nerves.

I closed my eyes. All this time, it had been me. Vincent and Edwin had seen the anomaly because I'd been with them in the forest. I must not have been close enough to Edwin to see it myself, that first time in 1912. I finished the lullaby, and heard Gaspery's applause.

He stood before me, clapping awkwardly. I was so embarrassed for him—for me? for us?—that it was difficult to meet his eyes, but I managed it. I was grateful that my dog had slept through my younger self's incompetence.

"Hello," he said brightly, in a jarringly imperfect accent. "My name's Gaspery-Jacques Roberts. I'm conducting some research on behalf of a music historian, and I wondered if I could possibly buy you some lunch."

13

"How would I describe my life?" I repeated, stalling. "Well, son, that's a big question. I don't know what I can tell you."

"Maybe you could tell me a little about what your days are like. If you don't mind. I haven't turned the recorder on yet, by the way. This is just us talking."

I nodded. I would keep him off-balance. I would quote Shakespeare at him because I knew he didn't know his Shakespeare yet. I would call him *son* because he hated being called *son*, and his irritation would distract him. I would bring up my dead wife because he was embarrassed by his own failed marriage. I would make him feel insecure about his accent, because accents and dialects were what he'd struggled with the most in his training. But first I would lull him with the quiet of my life.

"Well," I said. "I stand there for a few hours a day, playing the violin, while my dog naps at my feet, and the commuters dash by and throw change at me. They move with inhuman speed, the commuters. It took me some time to get used to this."

"Are you from around here?" the investigator asked.

"A farm just outside the city. Lived there all my life. But listen, son, by the time I took over the farm, small-scale farming had become mostly a matter of watching. You watch the robots move over the fields. You tinker with their settings sometimes but they're well made, they adjust themselves mostly, they don't need you for much. You play your violin in the field just to keep yourself occupied. In the distance the airships rise with the speed of fireflies, but they're faster up close."

When I played my violin at the airship terminal I sometimes thought it was as if the airships were falling upward, gravity reversed. They filled with a cargo of blank-faced commuters, then fell toward the sky. The commuters glanced at me sometimes as they passed, tossed coins into my hat. I watched their ships carry them up into the early morning, to jobs in Los Angeles, Nairobi, Edinburgh, Beijing. I thought of their souls moving fast through the morning sky.

"When my wife died," I told the investigator, "I kept up the farm for another year and then thought, to hell with it."

He was nodding, feigning interest, trying not to be nervous, trying to convince himself that he was doing a good job. What I didn't tell him: I felt that without Talia I might disappear into thin air, out there by myself. Just me and the dog and the farm robots, day after day. Loneliness wasn't a strong enough word for it. All that empty space. At night I sat on the porch with my dog, avoiding the silent house. Playing that game kids play, where you squint at the moon and half-convince yourself that you can see the brighter spots of the colonies on its surface. Distant over the fields, the lights of the city.

"Is it okay if I switch on the recorder?" the investigator asked.

"Go ahead."

"Okay, it's on. Thank you for taking the time to speak with me."

"You're welcome. Thank you for lunch."

"Now, just for the benefit of my recording, you're a violinist," my earlier self said.

I followed the script. "I am," I said. "I play in the airship terminal."

When I wasn't playing my violin in the airship terminal I liked to walk my dog in the streets between the towers. In those streets everyone moved faster than me, but what they didn't know was that I had already moved too fast, too far, and wished to travel no further. I've been thinking a great deal about time and motion lately, about being a still point in the ceaseless rush.

Notes and Acknowledgments

The quote referenced on page 72, "It's a great life if you don't weaken," is from John Buchan's 1919 novel *Mr. Standfast*.

The riff on page 95 re: chickens coming home to roost—"It's never good chickens"—is paraphrased from something the American poet Kay Ryan said when we were at a literary festival together in 2015.

The quote in the same chapter from the fourth-century Roman soldier and historian Ammianus Marcellinus, re: the Antonine Plague, is from Book XXIII of his writings, which are fascinating and available online.

I'm indebted to the books *Voyages of the* Columbia (ed. Frederic W. Howay) and *Scoundrels, Dreamers and Second Sons: British Remittance Men in the Canadian West*, by Mark Zuehlke.

With thanks to my agent, Katherine Fausset, and her colleagues at Curtis Brown; my editors—Jennifer Jackson at Knopf in New York City, Sophie Jonathan at Picador in London, and Jennifer Lambert at HarperCollins Canada in Toronto—and their colleagues; my U.K. agent, Anna Webber, and her colleagues at United Agents; Kevin Mandel, Rachel Fershleiser, and Semi Chellas, for reading and commenting on early drafts of this manuscript; and Michelle Jones, my daughter's nanny, for taking care of my daughter while I wrote this book.